"If and when I get married,"

Tessa's response was tart, "it will be to a man I not only know well enough to be sure of, but also respect!"

"Love not entering into it?"

"It's part and parcel."

Mark's mouth was sardonic. "Not always. You can know and respect without loving. Conversely, you can love without any finer feeling involved."

"You mean lust, don't you?" Her tone was biting. "It takes a man to confuse the two!"

"Made a study, have you?" He was already on his way out of the room, leaving her to follow on slowly. She would see this through whatever, Tessa vowed resolutely. She had no other choice.

KAY THORPE, an English author, has always been able to spin a good yarn. In fact, her teachers said she was the best storyteller in the school—particularly with excuses for being late! Kay then explored a few unsatisfactory career paths before giving rein to her imagination and hitting the jackpot with her first romance novel. After a roundabout route, she'd found her niche at last. The author is married with one son.

Books by Kay Thorpe

KAY THORPE
skin deep

Harlequin Books

TORONTO • NEW YORK • LONDON
AMSTERDAM • PARIS • SYDNEY • HAMBURG
STOCKHOLM • ATHENS • TOKYO • MILAN

Harlequin Presents first edition April 1990
ISBN 0-373-11261-0

Original hardcover edition published in 1989
by Mills & Boon Limited

Printed in U.S.A.

CHAPTER ONE

TESSA was half-way through her second cup of coffee when the telephone rang. She took the cup with her, balancing it somewhat precariously on the edge of the small shelf as she lifted the receiver.

The woman's voice cut across her automatic response. 'I knew you said you wanted a break after that last job, but this one could be something of a rest-cure in itself. Seven weeks right here in London looking after one child—how does that sound?'

'Too good not to have snags attached,' Tessa replied drily. 'And I was serious about that break. Those Reynolds children need a keeper more than they need a nanny!'

'You're the one who prefers the short-term jobs,' came the bland rejoinder. 'You can hardly expect to make much of an impression in a few weeks.'

Which was true enough, Tessa acknowledged. She had become too deeply attached to the very first child given into her charge, and been devastated when the family had returned to their home in the States. She could have gone with them, but the break would have had to come sooner or later. Since then she had concentrated on temporary positions, filling in where permanent nannies were ill or taking a holiday. The occasions on which there was no demand for her services were few and far between, hence the very real need for a rest before contemplating another job. Still, would it do any harm to find out what was entailed?

'Tell me about it,' she invited with a certain resignation.

'You'd be working for Mark Leyland, the travel writer,' said the woman on the other end of the line. 'He needs someone for the duration of the school holidays. The child is a boy, seven years old.'

'Surely the mother can cope with one small boy?'

'He's divorced.'

'So who normally looks after the child?'

'You'd have to ask him that yourself. If you're interested, I can give you the address to go along and see him. Only it has to be right away. School breaks on the twenty-second.'

Tessa glanced at the calendar pinned to the wall in front of her. 'That's the day after tomorrow!'

'I know. You're about his only hope.' The tone turned wheedling. 'He's offering double the usual salary.'

And double the normal agency rate too, no doubt, Tessa reflected. The money didn't particularly tempt her; she had more than enough stashed away for that rainy day. But the job itself sounded reasonable enough. Of course, she would have to find out more about it before she came to any hard and fast decision. The boy himself might prove to be a stumbling block. She had had enough of spoiled brats for the present.

'Is he going to be available this afternoon?' she asked.

'He said he'd be at home all day,' on a note of satisfaction. 'Do you have a pen handy?'

Tessa picked up the one attached to the notepad on the shelf. 'Fire away.'

It was a Kensington address. She could, Tessa reckoned, get close enough by tube to find the house itself on foot. It was almost lunch time now. If she left around two, that would be soon enough. No commitment, she reminded herself firmly. It all depended on what she found when she got there.

Lunch consisted of a cheese salad she had already prepared, together with a glass of the rather special red wine she had bought for last night's dinner. Mike hadn't stayed long enough to finish it. Nor had she wanted him to. From the first she had made it clear to him that friendship was all she had in mind where the two of them were concerned, but he hadn't been able to accept it that way. It was better that they parted. Better for both of them. Her job was what mattered most to her. Perhaps one day she might meet someone who meant even more, only there was plenty of time yet. Twenty-four wasn't exactly ancient.

She chose her outfit for the coming interview with care and precision, smoothing the skirt of the pale beige suit down over slender hips before donning the jacket. Her blouse was a deep cream, her only jewellery a gold chain at her throat. With mid-brown hair cut to fall neatly about her face, and the subtlest of make-up, she looked efficient without any suggestion of regimentation. Tessa hated uniforms. The first thing she had done on leaving the establishment where she had done her training was to stuff the grey and white garments that had been required for the course to the back of her wardrobe, where they had resided for the past three years.

The telephone rang again as she was about to leave the flat. Her mother sounded faint and faraway, as if she were calling from the other side of the world rather than Essex.

'What time are you planning on being here tomorrow?' she asked without preamble.

'Teatime-ish, I should think,' Tessa told her. 'Is it important?'

'Not especially.' Elizabeth Cadman's tone was over-casual. 'Just that Laura and Roger are coming over to dinner. They have a friend staying with them, so he'll be coming too. It will even up the numbers nicely.'

Matchmaking again, reflected Tessa with resigned tolerance. Neither her mother nor her sister could understand her lack of interest in settling down with some nice man. With her love of children, what better than to have some of her own? That was the question that most often cropped up. What she couldn't seem to get through to them was that one first had to meet Mr Right. She doubted very much if this friend of Laura and Roger's would turn out to be her soulmate. They never did. What her mother and sister thought she needed in a man was far different from her own ideal.

'I may not be able to spend the week as I planned after all,' she said. 'There's a new job in the offing. I'm on my way to an interview now.'

'Oh, but darling, you need the rest!' protested her mother. 'You haven't taken a real holiday in more than a year!'

'I know. Only this doesn't sound as if it's going to be any great hassle.'

'Where is it?'

'Kensington.' Tessa tagged on swiftly, 'Sorry, Mom, I really must go. I'll let you know what transpires. Bye for now.'

Her family meant well, she thought fondly as she replaced the receiver, but they worried far too much about her chosen way of life. She was going to come to little harm looking after other people's children, no matter what the circumstances.

The warm July sunshine was welcome after the ceaseless rain of the last week. Summer dresses were in vogue again. The journey across London was accomplished well within the hour she had allotted herself. By a quarter to three she was standing on the doorstep of number sixteen, Ranleigh Gardens, admiring the wide mahogany door with its gleaming brass while she waited for the bell to be answered.

Both downstairs windows had window-boxes over-flowing with red petunias. They made a vibrant splash of colour against the white walls. A woman's touch, Tessa reckoned. With a seven-year-old son, Mark Leyland was unlikely to be in his dotage himself; no doubt there were women still in his life. She wondered idly what might have caused the break-up of his mar-riage, then pulled herself up, because it was really none of her business.

When the door finally opened she had a composed smile all ready on her lips.

'Mr Leyland? I'm Tessa Cadman, from the agency.'

The tall, dark-haired man inclined his head in rec-ognition. 'You'd better come in.'

He closed the door behind her as she stepped through into the tastefully decorated hallway, opening another on his left and inviting her to enter. Tessa found herself in a large, high-ceilinged room that was a cross between study and library. Bookshelves lined the alcoves each side of the Adam-styled fireplace, filled to near capacity. There were piles of books too on the wide desk under the window, and stacked around the floor.

'Sorry about the mess,' proffered the man at her back. 'I'm having a sort-out. Sit down, won't you? No, over there,' as she started towards the desk. 'Let's be comfortable.'

Tessa took a seat on the chesterfield set at right angles to the fireplace, waiting until he had seated himself in one of the chairs opposite before saying levelly, 'I understand you need someone to look after your son while he's on holiday from school?'

'That's right,' he returned. 'Jason's seven. Too young to be left to fend for himself all day.'

'Much,' she agreed. She studied him for a moment, taking in the angular bone-structure, the taut jawline and firmly moulded mouth, coming back to meet deep-set grey eyes which returned her gaze without a flicker. 'Who takes care of him normally?'

'When he isn't in school, my housekeeper. Unfortunately, she had to leave us. With a new book to get out before the end of September, I obviously had to make other arrangements.'

'No one in the family who could help?'

'Apart from a brother right now overseas, there isn't any family.'

'You wouldn't consider postponing the book?'

One dark brow lifted sardonically. 'I was under the impression I was supposed to be interviewing *you*!'

Tessa kept her tone level. 'You're the one in most need, Mr Leyland. I can afford to be choosy. What other duties would I have?'

'Few,' he said. 'I have a woman who comes in three times a week to clean, and I mostly eat out myself. All you'd be called on to do is prepare your own and Jason's meals and keep him out of my hair while I work. If you think that's going to be too much for you——'

'I didn't say that.' Tessa could feel herself bristling and made an effort to retain her equilibrium. There was something about this man that rubbed her up the wrong way: the touch of arrogance in the tilt of the dark head, perhaps? 'Is Jason here now?'

'I'm due to pick him up in half an hour.' There was another pause, an obvious effort on his part to restart the conversation. 'Why don't you come along and meet him? It might help you make up your mind.'

Tessa was suddenly ashamed of her reservations. So what if she didn't feel particularly enamoured of the father? It was the son who had to be considered the most. 'That would be nice,' she acknowledged. 'Is the school far?'

'A few minutes by car. We don't have to leave until twenty to.' He stirred himself. 'Would you like some tea?'

'Please.' She hesitated before tagging on tentatively, 'Perhaps I could make it?'

Already on his feet, he gave her a derisive glance. 'I'm capable of pouring boiling water on to a few tea-leaves.'

Brown eyes returned the derision. 'I use tea-bags myself. No sugar, thank you, and just a drop of milk.'

Almost imperceptibly his lips twitched. 'Five minutes,' he promised.

Left alone in the quiet room, Tessa got to her feet to look at the book titles crowding the nearest shelves. Most were non-fiction, none of them books on travel. Those were in the other section on the far side of the fireplace. Several carried the name Mark Leyland along the spine. She had heard of him, of course, although she had never read him. Taking up one on the Caribbean, she flicked through the pages, pausing here and there to scan a few lines. Nothing dry about this prose, she was bound to acknowledge. His descriptions of both places and people conjured vivid pictures in the mind's eye.

She was still reading when the author returned, bearing a loaded tray. Putting the book unhurriedly back on the shelf, she returned to her seat to watch him pour the fragrant brew into the two fine china cups.

'Add your own milk,' he invited, selecting one of the cups for himself. 'Biscuit to go with it—or are you on a permanent diet?'

'I'm lucky,' she returned equably. 'I have a fast metabolism, so I don't need to bother.'

She took a sip of the hot tea, unsurprised to find that it tasted as good as it looked. Mark Leyland no doubt performed every task he set himself with care, precision and total success. He was that kind of man. Once again she found herself wondering why his wife had left him, only to catch herself up at the unfairness of that assumption. For all she knew, the boot had been on the other foot. Except that, if so, it was unusual for him to have custody of the child. Unusual in either case, in point of fact. The mother would normally be granted such rights as a matter of course.

'Are you planning on finding another housekeeper?' she heard herself asking.

'It depends,' he said. 'Good ones are few and far between.' The grey eyes held a faint light of mockery. 'I understand you only take on temporary jobs yourself. Scared of commitment?'

'Of involvement,' she corrected smoothly. 'It's too easy to become attached and cause pain both sides when the time comes to leave.'

'You should get married and have a couple of kids of your own. That way you wouldn't have to leave them.'

She laughed. 'Now you sound like my mother!'

'Sensible woman. It's the obvious solution.'

Stung, she said sharply, 'I'd have thought you'd be one of the last to advocate marriage as a way of life, Mr Leyland.'

'Because mine broke up?' He registered the slight run of colour under her skin with a twist of his lips. 'Don't worry, I'm not all that sensitive about it.'

'All the same, I shouldn't have said it,' Tessa apologised.

'You wouldn't be female if you weren't curious,' he came back on a dry note. 'For the record, she left Jason with me voluntarily when she went. I didn't have to fight for him. Not that I wouldn't have done. He's a great kid.'

'I'm sure of it.' Her voice had softened. 'It can't have been easy for you.'

Something in him seemed to close up. When he spoke again it was on an unemotional level. 'We should be thinking about leaving. Jason tends to get worried if someone isn't there to collect him on the dot.'

That was something Tessa could appreciate. A child deprived of one parent was likely to develop a fear of total abandonment. She would have liked to know how long it had been since Jason had seen his mother, but didn't care to put the question. It was obvious that Mark Leyland already regretted what little he had told her.

The silver-grey XJ40 parked opposite the front door proved to be their mode of travel. Seated at his side, Tessa drew pleasurably on the smell of leather. No more than a few months old, at a guess. Writing travel books must be a pretty lucrative occupation, considering Mark Leyland's standard of living—especially if he was also paying maintenance to his ex-wife. Curiosity again, she chided herself. All the same, it was difficult not to wonder what the former Mrs Leyland was like. Living with a man of his type couldn't be easy. He would want his 't's crossed and 'i's dotted all along the line!

As he had said, it took only minutes to reach the private school where his son was undergoing preparatory education. He left her sitting in the car while he went to fetch the child.

Tessa had opportunity to study the two of them as they came back across the forecourt. Fair-haired, and quite small of stature, Jason bore little immediately apparent resemblance to his father. He seemed to have little of a seven-year-old's usual exuberance, piling obediently into the rear of the car on reaching it.

'Hello, Jason,' she said, half turning in her seat to smile at him. 'Had a good day?'

There was a certain reticence in the bright blue regard. 'Yes, thank you,' he answered politely. 'Daddy says you're coming to stay with us.'

'That's right.' Tessa avoided glancing in his father's direction as the latter slid behind the wheel. Had she not already made the decision, it would, it appeared, have been made for her. She wasn't sure how she felt about that. Telling the child amounted to emotional blackmail, in effect. A man accustomed to having his way, that was Mark Leyland. Only he had better watch out, because she was no pushover when it came to a battle of wills. 'I'm looking forward to it,' she added. 'You'll have to start thinking about things you'd like to do and see this summer.'

He considered the question quite seriously for a moment. 'I don't mind,' he acknowledged at length, 'as long as I don't have to go to boarding-school next term.'

'It isn't always possible to arrange things the way we'd like,' put in his father without taking his eyes from the road ahead. 'Sometimes it's necessary to accept changes.'

'I don't want to go.' There was anxiety in that statement.

A faint compression appeared momentarily about Mark Leyland's mouth. 'We'll talk about it later.'

Tessa bit down hard on the urge to put in her spoke. No long-term involvement, she reminded herself. She would be in charge of Jason for a few short weeks. What happened after that was none of her concern.

All the same, she felt sorry for the boy. He was caught in a situation not of his own making. How any woman could walk out on her own child was beyond reckoning. Even if she had felt she was no longer able to live with the man she had married, she must surely have felt *something* for their only son!

'You'll stay for tea?' Mark Leyland asked when they reached the house again. 'Nothing elaborate. Jason has a hot lunch in school.'

And how would they be coping for the coming couple of days? Tessa wondered. There were always restaurants, of course, but that was hardly ideal with a seven-year-old in tow. She would be willing to bet they'd just make do with what was in the house, the way her father would if left to his own devices. From the look of him, her new employer was no self-indulger in rich food, anyway. Healthily lean and lithe was the phrase that sprang to mind, his arms taut-muscled beneath the short-sleeved shirt. Probably kept himself in trim at the local gym. She placed him at around thirty-three or -four, so he would have been no callow youth when he married. Unless, of course, Jason had not come on the scene until several years after. He might even have been unplanned—unwanted by the mother, if not the father. That could explain a lot.

She realised suddenly that he was still waiting for her answer, brow raised as he studied her face. 'Thank you, I'd like to,' she said hurriedly. 'Only this time I'll do the honours. If I'm going to be working for you, I may as well make a start.'

'If you really mean that, you could move in right away,' he said. 'Give you time to find your bearings before school breaks, and help me out. I'm having lunch with my publisher tomorrow. Getting away in time to collect Jason from school might present a problem.'

Jason was already out of the car and waiting patiently on the front step. Looking at the small figure, Tessa knew she was lost. Laura would simply have to entertain their guest herself.

'I don't see why not,' she said slowly, aware of an odd reluctance even as she did so. 'I could be here before noon.'

'What's wrong with tonight?' he came back. 'We could run you over to wherever it is you live and collect your things.'

'There are all kinds of arrangements I have to make myself,' she protested. 'I only got back from my last job a few days ago.'

'You live alone?'

'No.' Faced with the steady scrutiny, she felt somehow bound to enlarge on that bare statement of fact. 'I pay a nominal rent to my flatmate when I'm not in residence, a full share when I am. It's an arrangement that suits us both. Right now she's away herself.'

'So where's the problem? I'll cover any rent you're due to make up—in addition to salary, of course.'

'That wasn't what I meant.' Tessa made a helpless little gesture. 'There are papers to cancel—milk—packing to do.'

'You can go back at the weekend to do the bulk,' her new employer pointed out with determination. 'I need you now.'

The knock on the side window broke into her reply. Jason had come back to the car to see what was keeping them, his expression curious as he peered in. 'Are you coming, Daddy?'

The latter opened his door. 'We both are. Miss Cadman is staying to tea.'

'Tessa,' she corrected, getting out of the far side of the car to look across the long, low bonnet at the two standing on the pavement. 'Call me Tessa, please.'

'Better if we dispense with formality altogether, so make it Mark.' He was smiling now, obviously satisfied that he had won the day. 'Let's go on in.'

The name suited him, she thought irrelevantly as she moved in the wake of father and son. From the rear he looked taller than ever, broad in the shoulder and narrow of waist and hip. His hair was thick, with the merest hint of a wave in its crisp styling. An attractive man, if one liked the clipped, impersonal type.

He turned her loose in the beautifully equipped kitchen without objection once he had relieved her of her jacket. There was a freezer full of food, and plenty of stored dry goods in the walk-in larder. Jason came into the room while she was still in the process of contemplating the alternatives, perching on a stool to watch her as she browsed through the cupboards.

'Do you have any special likes or dislikes?' she asked without turning her head.

'I hate peas,' he declared.

'Right, so we don't have peas.' She looked at him then, expression enquiring. 'How about favourites?'

A smile lit the well-formed features. 'Chilli con carne.'

'Really? That's one of mine, too. What about your father?'

There was a sudden reassuring gleam of mischief in the blue eyes. 'He always says I shouldn't be faddy about food.'

'Does he?' Tessa grinned back conspiratorially. 'Then we'll all have chilli. I'll have to use the microwave to defrost the mince. In fact, I'll cook the whole thing in there. It's going to take too long otherwise.'

'We usually just have sandwiches,' Jason confided. 'Since Mrs Kiveton left, anyway.'

'I expect you'll be having a new housekeeper eventually,' said Tessa on a light note.

At that precise moment, with his expression suddenly blanked, there was a certain resemblance to his father. 'I don't know.'

Tessa wondered fleetingly why this Mrs Kiveton had left, but had no intention of indulging the curiosity. The more she became involved in the Leylands' lives, the harder it would be to stand aside when the time came. A great kid, Mark had said of his son. So far she saw no cause to dispute that assessment. He was the kind who could all too easily crawl up under the skin and lodge there.

Jason disappeared again while she was defrosting the mince. Perhaps to warn his father of the culinary delights to come, she thought whimsically. Chilli might not be considered the ideal tea-time treat, but if it was what her charge wanted it was what he was going to get, regardless. She had a feeling that treats were few and far between where this child was concerned.

There was a sizeable breakfast-room next door to the kitchen. She set three places at the round table under the window, looking out at the paved courtyard with its flower-filled troughs and spilling profusion of plant life. Not much room for a boy to play, she reflected. Not much scope for imagination, either. He needed trees to climb, streams to dam, even a patch of earth that was all his own to till and tend and grow things in. As a writer, Mark Leyland could work anywhere, so why stick to the city? There were good schools within reach of the Surrey or Kentish countryside.

She found Jason sprawled on the floor watching television in the large and lovely drawing-room. His father, he said, was in the study. Tessa tapped on the partially opened door, poking her head round it in response to the somewhat distracted invitation.

'Supper's ready,' she announced. 'Are you?'

Mark looked up from the desk where he appeared to be working on some papers. For a moment he seemed almost puzzled, as if he had forgotten her presence in the house, then his brow cleared.

'I thought it was supposed to be tea.'

'Supper suits the timing better,' she returned blandly. 'Come and get it while it's hot.'

Jason was already seated at the table when she wheeled in the loaded trolley. Mark followed her in, taking his place next to his son while Tessa ladled generous helpings of rice and chilli on to a plate.

'Good lord,' he said blankly when she set it down in front of him.

Tessa shared a glance wth his son. 'You don't like chilli?'

'I can't——' He looked up suddenly to catch the smile on the boy's face, his own mouth widening reluctantly as realisation struck home. 'Hoist with my own petard!' he murmured, and then, on a rather brusquer note to Tessa herself, 'That's sheer indulgence.'

'I know.' She was not about to be put down. 'There's no harm in a little indulgence from time to time.'

Grey eyes regarded her with slightly narrowed intent. 'Is that what they taught you at your training school— assuming you did go to training school?'

'Yes to both questions.' She gave Jason his plate, setting her own down at the empty place and sliding into her seat. 'Do we say grace?'

'We do in school,' piped up the younger member of the Leyland family as his father hesitated.

'Then perhaps you'd like to say it for us now,' invited Tessa.

Jason did so, clearly and concisely, taking up his knife and fork the moment the 'Amen' was out of the way. He didn't pick at his food, but his manners were impeccable. His father tasted with caution before nodding somewhat surprised approval in Tessa's direction.

'It's good! Not too hot.'

From the way he tucked in, a sandwich tea would have scarcely sufficed. Tessa could only regret that she hadn't cooked double the quantity.

'I didn't prepare a pudding,' she said, tongue in cheek, when they had scraped the platters clean between them, 'but I noticed some ice-cream in the freezer, and there's no shortage of tinned fruit, if that would be acceptable?'

It was Jason who did the answering, with enthusiasm. 'Scrummy!'

Mark settled for coffee as an alternative. They drank it out in the courtyard after Tessa had loaded the dishwasher.

'That was the best chilli I ever tasted,' he conceded, mellowed by the warmth of the evening sun, the fragrance from the surrounding flower troughs. 'At the very least, Jason isn't going to starve this next few weeks. Playing father *and* mother to a seven-year-old is no sinecure!'

'Losing your housekeeper will have caused you a lot of problems,' Tessa sympathised, and saw the broad shoulders lift.

'She had family problems of her own. Just one of those things.'

If he really were planning on sending Jason to boarding-school, he could probably save himself the trouble of seeking a new housekeeper by moving to a more easily managed home, reflected Tessa fleetingly. Aloud, she said with purpose, 'If we're going to get over to my place and back again before Jason's bed time, shouldn't we be thinking about moving?'

'He's on holiday,' Mark pointed out. 'A late night won't hurt him for once.'

'All the same——' she was stubbornly disinclined to let him have his way '—I'd prefer to get it done with.'

She could feel his eyes on her as she got to her feet. When he spoke it was with deceptive softness. 'I've no need of a governess.'

Her own tone was just as soft. 'And I've no actual *need* of a job just now.'

A corner of the strong mouth turned down. 'Are you threatening to withdraw your services?'

'Not unless you make it impossible for me to work for you. You were the one,' she added before he could speak, 'who suggested I move in tonight. I'd as soon have waited until tomorrow.'

'Point taken.' He was on his feet as he said it, face expressionless. 'I'll round Jason up.'

Don't sulk about it, Tessa wanted to say, except that sulk was the wrong word. Mark Leyland was accustomed to ruling the roost in his own home—and no doubt elsewhere too—only not with her. She had started as she meant to go on. He could accept it, or he could do the other thing.

CHAPTER TWO

IT WAS almost seven-thirty by the time they reached the flat just off the Edgware Road. Unable to leave the two of them sitting in the car while she organised herself, Tessa took them up with her.

'Make yourselves at home,' she invited in the little lobby, throwing open the door to the living-room. 'I'll be as quick as I can.'

The bedroom she shared on occasion with Barbara, her flatmate, was large and airy. Converted though it was into flats, the house itself was similar in overall size to the Leyland residence. Why one man and a child should need a place that big defied reason, thought Tessa fleetingly, taking out the suitcase she had only unpacked a few short days ago and opening it up on her bed. Just enough to last over the weekend, then she could come back for more.

Mark was leafing through a book of aerial views when she went through, while Jason amused himself with the Newton's cradle executive toy standing on one of the low tables Barbara seemed to collect by the half-dozen.

'I like this,' he announced. 'Can we have one, Daddy?'

'*May* we have one,' corrected his father, closing the book. 'And the answer is no. It doesn't serve any useful purpose.'

'It's supposed to relieve tension,' Tessa said mildly, and received an ironic glance.

'And does it?'

'I don't know,' she admitted. 'I'm never tense.'

'Never?' The irony increased. 'You must be one of the few.'

Was, she thought with an irony of her own. There was tension in her at this moment, and for no good reason. What was it about this man that put her so much on edge?

'Ready?' he asked now.

'Just a note to write for Barbara—she's due back on Friday—and another for the milkman. I can phone the newsagent in the morning.' She was seeking out pen and paper as she spoke. 'The rent's paid, so there's no problem there.' Scribbling a few lines, she added casually, 'Bring that with you if you want to, Jason. Barbara won't mind you borrowing it for a spell.'

'I do,' stated Mark firmly. 'Leave it, Jason. You've plenty of toys of your own at home.'

Jason obeyed reluctantly. Tessa bit her lip. She had been wrong to proffer the invitation without prior consultation, perhaps, but Mark could surely have stretched a point for once? They would have to come to some kind of understanding over demarcation lines. There was no way she was going to go seeking permission to proceed every time the child expressed an interest in anything.

With the notes written, there was no further excuse to linger. Mark carried her suitcase down to the car and stashed it away in the boot. To any passer-by they might well be a family group setting out on a long weekend, reflected Tessa as he slid his long frame in beside her. Not that she would want to be married to a man like Mark Leyland. No way!

Jason fell asleep in the back on the way home. 'Bed for you,' declared Tessa when they were indoors. 'I'll run the bath while you undress. Just show me the way.' To Mark she added, 'If you'll drop my suitcase there in the hall, I can take it up myself later.'

'May as well do it now,' he said, making for the stairs. 'You can have the room next to Jason's, and share the same bathroom.'

She followed him up, Jason between them. Half-way along the broad landing he threw open a door on the right. 'This is you. Jason is the next door along, the bathroom the one after that. I'm in the master suite along at the end.' He moved forward into the room to lift her suitcase on to the double bed. 'It's kept made-up ready for unexpected guests, so you should find everything you need.' Grey eyes moved from her to the small, sleepy figure of his son hovering in the doorway. 'I think we can skip the bath tonight.'

'If you say so.' Tessa was not about to argue that decision. She smiled at the child. 'I'll come and tuck you in when you're ready.'

Jason looked intrigued by the offer. 'All right,' he said. 'Night, Daddy.'

Mark made no move towards him. 'Goodnight.'

'Don't molly-coddle him,' he added coolly to Tessa when the boy had gone. 'He's seven years old, not three. He hardly needs tucking in!'

'It's a figure of speech,' she responded, borrowing his tone. 'The actual act went out with the advent of duvets. I'll simply be going in to say goodnight.'

'You could have done that here and now.'

'The way you did?' She shook her head. 'He isn't too old for a goodnight kiss—especially from his parent. You won't make him soft by showing affection.'

His regard had hardened. 'You've been with us less than six hours. Would you say that was long enough to make unqualified judgements?'

Mentally Tessa squared her shoulders. 'It took me less than one hour to realise you're trying to make him grow up too fast and too soon. I sympathise with your position. As I already said, it can't have been easy.' The hesitation was brief. 'How long has his mother been gone?'

The answer came terse. 'Four years.'

'He hasn't seen her in all that time?'

Firm lips twisted. 'If she'd had any feeling for him at all, do you think she'd have left him in the first place?'

Tessa said evenly, 'That rather depends on her reasons for leaving.'

His eyes were like flint. 'Is a family case history a prime requisite of your job?'

'No, but it helps to know what kind of situation I'm up against.' She made a semi-apologetic little gesture. 'I'm sorry if I appeared to be prying into your affairs. I'm only concerned for Jason's welfare.'

'For a few weeks,' he pointed out. 'After that it won't be your problem. No involvement, I think you said?'

He was right, Tessa was bound to acknowledge. She was breaking one of her own golden rules, the reason being that this job was already proving different from others she had taken on. She felt close to Jason, ready to defend his rights. His father loved him, she was certain, but he had little understanding of a child's needs. If in the coming weeks she could help him adjust his attitude, that would at least be something. Boarding-school was no answer. Jason needed the warmth and security of a loving home. Mark should get married again—and soon.

'I remember,' she said.

'Then act on it.' He moved on past her to the door, expression austere. 'I've some work to do.'

'Shall I bring you a hot drink in later?' she ventured, and braced herself for the flash of derision as he turned his head back towards her again.

'If I want one, I'll get it myself. I don't expect you to wait on either of us hand and foot.'

How about knees? she almost flashed back, but restrained the impulse. There was nothing to be gained from childish repartee.

Left alone, she found time for a swift but comprehensive scrutiny of the room that was to be hers for the next few weeks. It left, she had to admit, little to be desired in the way of home comforts. The furnishings were of old pine waxed to a warm glow, the fabrics and wall coverings a Laura Ashley design blending all the autumnal colours. Thick carpeting in golden brown sprang underfoot.

There was no dust on the surfaces. Obviously the domestic help did a thorough job, because she couldn't for a moment imagine Mark Leyland wielding a duster. In any case, she was more than capable of a little housework herself.

Jason was already in bed when she put her head round his door, fair head small and defenceless on the pillow. The room was beautifully and very suitably decorated in primary colours, with lots of shelf space for the dozens of books and toys all neatly arranged. What money could buy he had in abundance, thought Tessa in swift appraisement. Indulgence of a kind, but lacking in soul.

'You keep your things very tidy,' she commented on a light note, approaching the bed.

'If I put one thing away before getting another out, it's easy,' he responded in the manner of one repeating a well-learned lesson. 'Are you going to tuck me in now?'

'Soon.' She added tentatively, 'Would you like me to read to you for a while first?'

Blue eyes showed sudden indignation. '*I* can read!'

'I'm sure you read very well,' she agreed, 'but it's nice sometimes to just lie back and listen instead.' She cast a glance along the nearest shelf. 'How about *The Wind in The Willows*? I like that one.'

'All right.' He was humouring her, that was apparent from his expression. 'The bit where Ratty and Mole get lost in the Wild Wood and find Mr Badger's house, please.'

Tessa smiled at him. 'I'm impressed! Have you read the whole book?'

'Not every word,' he said quite seriously. 'Some of them are a bit long. I like Toad best,' he tagged on in sudden confidence. 'He's funny!'

'My favourite is Otter,' Tessa confessed. 'I love the way he just disappears in the middle of a sentence.' She sat down on the edge of the mattress, riffling through the pages to find the chapter she wanted. 'Let's start where the two of them find the doorscraper, shall we?'

She read for almost ten minutes, delighted to see Jason's interest captured, to hear his chuckle when she played Mole being first obtuse and then so over-effusive. She sensed the moment when his eyes started to grow heavy, but continued to read until she was sure he was fully asleep.

Closing the book softly, she laid it to one side, then bent on impulse to press a light kiss on the downy cheek. The Reynolds children, who had been her previous charges, had driven her to distraction with their antics, and been all too easy to leave. Jason was another matter altogether. Already he was casting a net about her heart.

The door to the study was closed when she went down after unpacking her things. It was barely ten o'clock, and dusk was only just falling. She sat out in the courtyard for a while, enjoying the tranquillity of the evening, then made herself a drink and a sandwich in the kitchen. At eleven, when she finally decided to retire for the night, the study door was still firmly closed. So be it, she thought.

She had been asleep what seemed like bare minutes when she was awoken again by the sound of a child crying out. Jason was sitting up in bed when she reached him, his eyes huge and dark in his pinched little face.

'Did you have a bad dream?' Tessa soothed, stroking the damp hair away from his forehead. 'It's all right now, darling, it's gone.'

'I don't want to go away to school.' His voice trembled as if tears were not so far away. 'I'll hate it there!'

'How can you tell before you've even been?' asked his father from the doorway. 'You're letting imagination run away with you.'

The anxiety remained in his son's eyes. '*Are* you going to send me away, Daddy?'

There was hesitation in the reply. 'It depends what we come up with. Anyway, you'd enjoy it once you got there. You'd have lots of friends to play with.' His tone altered, became authoritative again. 'Now come on, lie down and go back to sleep. There's no point in worrying about something that hasn't even happened yet.'

Tessa drew the cover up around the boy as he subsided obediently into bed, stifling the urge to whisper reassurances in his ear. Mark Leyland was an unfeeling brute, and she was prepared to tell him so to his face, but it wasn't her place to usurp his authority in front of his son. There had to be another answer for a child as sensitive as Jason. There simply had to be!

Mark waited with a hand on the doorknob until she was clear of the room, closing the door in her wake with a firm click. He must have been in the bath or shower, she realised, turning to face him. His only covering appeared to be the towelling robe. Grey eyes regarded her coolly.

'Something to say, have you?'

She saw no point in denial. 'Only that I find your attitude a little too unsympathetic. A housekeeper as substitute mother is hardly ideal, but at least there's an element of security in familiar surroundings. You could totally undermine his confidence by forcing an issue he's so obviously against!'

It was a moment before he replied, his expression controlled. 'I think you and I had better get a few things sorted out before we go any further. Shall we go downstairs where Jason can't overhear us?'

Tessa bit her lip, aware that he had a point. A child's ears were sharp; certainly a closed door was no real barrier. All the same, she had no intention of relinquishing her stand. Jason needed someone to fight for his rights, it was obvious.

Her own wrap was a cotton print more practical than pretty. Fleetingly, and irrelevantly, she found herself regretting that fact. Mark was close behind her as they descended to the lower floor, his hand closing on the hall light switch at the same moment that she located it. Brief though it was, the contact sent a tingle like a small electric shock down the length of her arm. Static, she thought. Just plain old static. It could scarcely be anything else.

He indicated the study, following her in to switch on a lamp. In the soft light he seemed to tower.

'So you disapprove of boarding-schools,' he stated flatly. 'Any valid reason?'

'I didn't say I disapproved,' Tessa denied. 'Not in general. I just don't happen to believe Jason a suitable candidate, that's all. Not at present, anyway.'

He leaned his weight against the desk edge to regard her with a line drawn between dark brows, the bathrobe wrapped across strong brown thighs. 'Your training includes a degree in psychology, by any chance?'

She refused to allow the sarcasm to deflect her. 'One hardly needs paper qualifications to see what should be obvious even to the untrained eye.

The frown deepened. 'Are you suggesting I've no interest in my son's welfare?'

'I'm suggesting you might not have given enough thought to his emotional needs. It isn't deprivation that makes the man.'

'Is that a fact?' There was a sudden hard gleam of mockery in the grey eyes. 'My work involves a great deal of travel. I can't take him with me, and I doubt if I'm going to find another Mrs Kiveton in a hurry, so what would be *your* solution?'

'You should get married again.'

One eyebrow flicked upwards. 'Anyone in mind?'

The taunt registered but was ignored. Tessa gave him back look for look. 'Obviously not. But I don't imagine you've become a misogynist, either.'

'No, I don't suppose I have. On the other hand, I don't know anyone ready to become instant mother to a seven-year-old boy.'

Which didn't necessarily mean he hadn't contemplated remarriage, reasoned Tessa. Perhaps there were factors other than those stated for sending the child away to boarding-school? She wondered fleetingly if he had ever made any attempt to contact his ex-wife, then dismissed the thought as irrelevant to the present question.

'It's quite a problem,' she agreed. 'But I still think Jason's welfare should come before anything else.'

His scrutiny was slow and measured, taking in every detail of her face. Tessa returned the gaze with a calm that was all surface, aware of her suddenly heightened pulse-rate, of a tension that seemed to start in the very pit of her stomach and spread upwards into her chest. The white robe had sprung open a little above the waist; she could see the swirl of dark hair, sense the lean muscularity.

'You're not consistent,' he observed. 'You tell me you dislike involvement, yet what would you call this?'

Her shrug was as light as she could make it. 'Wasn't it Emerson who said "consistency is the hobgoblin of little minds"?'

'Ralph Waldo left quotes to cover every occasion,' came the dry retort, 'but it doesn't answer the question. Why single Jason out for special interest?'

Her eyes acquired a sudden spark. 'Perhaps because I feel a special sympathy for the innocent victims of a divorce. The children are the ones who suffer most every time!'

'Except that in his case, Jason scarcely remembers his mother.' The tone was quiet but with an underlying steeliness that bespoke held-in anger. 'Are your own parents divorced, by any chance?'

'No, they're not. They had their silver wedding five years ago.'

'They were lucky.'

'Not *just* luck. They worked at it. Few marriages are made in heaven.'

'That's definitely not Emerson. Get some experience under your belt, and you'll have room to talk!'

'*If* and *when* I get married,' she responded tartly, 'it will be to a man I not only know well enough to be sure of, but also respect!'

'Love not entering into it?'

'It's part and parcel.'

His mouth was sardonic. 'Not always. You can know and respect without loving. Conversely, you can love without any finer feeling involved.'

'You mean lust, don't you?' Her tone bit. 'It takes a man to confuse the two!'

'Made a study, have you?'

This time she was unable to hold his gaze, lowering hers to the region of his throat. 'It doesn't take any expertise.'

'No,' he agreed, 'just a damned cynical little mind!' He straightened abruptly. 'I think we'd better get back to bed. Separately, of course, just in case you're thinking the lust might be extended in your direction.'

'It wouldn't have occurred to me,' she denied. 'I'm about as far removed from your kind of woman as you are from my kind of man!'

'That's the closest you've come to discernment.' He added hardily, 'If it weren't for the fact that I'm unlikely to find anyone else to fill the position at such short notice, we'd be parting company in the morning. Uninformed criticism I can do without.'

Tessa's chin lifted. 'I could make the decision for you, if you like.'

'If you're as concerned for Jason's welfare as you make out, that's an empty threat.' He paused, infuriating in his cool control. 'I'll be going out quite early, so we may not see each other until evening. That should give us both time to come to terms with the idea of compromise. It's only for a few weeks. We should be able to cope that long.'

He might; Tessa doubted her own ability. He was right about one thing, though: she couldn't desert Jason. What was to happen at the end of the summer was an unanswered question as yet. If the boarding-school idea was to be taken up, it would surely be necessary to make arrangements well in advance of the new term? There were such things as entrance examinations, for in-

stance—unless Mark had enough influence to waive such
considerations.

He was already on his way out of the room, leaving
her to follow on slowly behind. She would see this
through whatever, she vowed resolutely. She had no other
choice.

There was plenty of time over the following days to ac-
custom herself to the house and immediate surroundings. Mark was out for most meals, which made
things easier. On the few occasions when she did find
herself alone with him, conversation was limited to the
purely impersonal from both sides.

Her relationship with Jason progressed by leaps and
bounds. She was building up heartache for herself, she
knew, but she couldn't hold back. Children fortunately
had short memories. He might miss her when she went,
but he would soon forget. It wasn't like losing a parent.
She was going to be the one who suffered most from the
parting.

She took him with her when she went to visit her own
family on the Tuesday. Her mother was captivated by
the son, and curious to the point of intrigue about the
father.

'I've read his books, of course,' she declared. 'You
know how fascinated I've always been by travel. A
widower, is he?'

Tessa sighed, acknowledging that her resolution to say
nothing about her new employer outside of the basic
facts had been so much wishful thinking. 'He's divorced.'

'Oh?' For a moment Elizabeth Cadman looked dis-
appointed, then she rallied again. 'Well, I suppose there's
little stigma attached these days, no matter who was at
fault.'

'*She* left *him*,' Tessa felt bound to state, and was immediately cross with herself because it sounded as if she were defending him. 'Anyway, it's of no real importance, except to Jason.'

The latter had gone for a walk with her father and the family dog. Watching the small figure stepping out, lead in hand, hearing his voice chatting away, she had cautiously congratulated herself on having managed to undermine that 'only child' reserve. He was lonely, that was the main trouble. He needed companionship. As a boarder he would have friends constantly about him. Would it really be such a bad thing?

Yes, but it wasn't the same as a family and home, another part of her mind retaliated. For too long he had been foisted off on other people. He needed a stable environment. It was time Mark did something about finding himself another wife.

'He's a very attractive man, isn't he?' her mother said now on an over-casual note, drawing her attention back to earth with a jerk.

'How do you know that?'

'There was a photograph of him on the dustcover of his last book. Early thirties, it said.'

'Oh, a talking picture!'

Mrs Cadman ignored the satire. 'I meant the bit underneath. He must have been quite young when they were married. How long has he been divorced?'

Tessa stifled a further sigh. It was more than obvious where all these questions were leading. 'Long enough to have acquired a taste for bachelorhood,' she said. 'So if you're thinking of him as possible husband material for me, forget it, Mom.' She softened the impact with a smile. 'I'm not really all that desperate to find a man.'

The other was unimpressed by the denial. 'I'd got Laura and was expecting you when I was twenty-four.'

She studied her daughter in exasperation. 'You don't make the most of yourself, you know. If you'd have your hair cut short and bubbly, and use a little more make-up——'

'I still wouldn't have your and Laura's looks.' Tessa said it without rancour, too long aware of her short-comings to feel any pain. 'And bubbles are out.'

'At your age you should have the confidence to be yourself and ignore fashion,' came the response.

'That's what I'm trying to be—when I'm allowed.' She made another attempt, knowing it was useless even as she said it. 'Mom, there are plenty of women who never get married and still manage to live full and useful lives.'

'Is that what you want?'

'Not necessarily. But I could settle for it if I had to.'

'But that's just what I'm trying to tell you—you don't have to. You'd make a wonderful wife and mother!'

'Which still leaves the missing ingredient.' Tessa shook her head. 'You were lucky. You met Dad. They don't come like him too often.'

The velvety dark brown eyes mother had passed on to both daughters softened reminiscently. 'Perhaps not. Still, Laura didn't do too badly with Roger.'

Visualising her handsome brother-in-law, Tessa was forced to concede that point. Roger might well have sown some wild oats in his younger days, but now, at thirty-two, was the devoted family man without apparent regrets.

'Anyway,' Elizabeth concluded comfortably, not about to relinquish all hope, 'you'll be spending the next few weeks together.'

If not exactly in harmony, Tessa reflected drily. If this morning's visitor was anything to go by, Mark's taste in women ran to the blonde and beautiful, which left her

right out of the running stakes even if she had har-
boured any hopes in his direction.

Judging from the expression on the smoothly lovely
face when she had opened the door, her own presence
in the house had not been anticipated.

'Do I take it you're the new housekeeper?' the woman
asked with an odd inflection after being advised that Mr
Leyland was not at home. 'You're very young!'

How old did one need to be? wondered Tessa. 'I'm
Jason's nanny,' she said. 'Is there any message I can give
Mr Leyland?'

'I'd better write him one,' said the other, stepping
confidently over the threshold. 'I'm going to be out of
town for the next couple of days, so he won't be able
to contact me. If that's coffee I can smell, I'd love a
cup!'

Not a first visit by any means, Tessa concluded as she
disappeared into the study. Shrugging, she closed the
front door again and went to pour a second cup of coffee.
Jason was playing in his room until she was ready to
leave. Hopefully, the newcomer would be on her way as
soon as she had drunk her coffee, or they were going to
be late for lunch. Ten-thirty in the morning was an odd
time to come visiting, anyway.

The latter was seated at the desk using notepad and
pen when she went into the study.

'I'll leave it right here where he's sure to see it,' she
declared, tearing off the sheet and folding it. 'Is that
mine?'

Tessa took the cup across to the desk, quelling the
urge to tell the woman where she got off. About twenty-
eight, she judged, and possessed of a nerve second to
none.

'So you're going to be looking after Jason,' said the other, leaning back in the chair. 'On a permanent basis, is that?'

'Actually, no,' Tessa returned levelly. 'Just the summer.'

'Ah!' There was a certain satisfaction in the pale blue eyes. 'I hope you realise Mr Leyland needs peace and quiet while he's writing?'

'He'll have it,' Tessa assured her. 'I'll be keeping Jason fully occupied one way or another.'

'That's good. Children are a distraction at the best of times.'

Tessa kept a tight rein on her tongue. She just wished the woman would hurry up and go. So far she didn't even know her name. One didn't, she gathered, introduce oneself to the hired help.

Jason appeared in the doorway, his eager expression altering abruptly when he saw the visitor. Tessa thought she saw panic in his eyes for a fleeting moment before they went dull and blank.

'Hello, Jason,' smiled the other woman on a note that sounded, to Tessa's ears at least, totally insincere. 'I hope you're going to be a good boy for your father while he's working this summer.'

'Yes, I will, Mrs Hammond.' His voice was flat, his whole demeanour altered from the child Tessa had come to know and love this past week. 'Is Daddy here too?'

'No, I just popped in to leave him a message.' She finished the coffee and rose to her feet, her glance coming back to Tessa, cool and composed. 'Make sure he gets it, won't you? Don't bother to see me out. I know the way well enough.'

Jason stepped back into the hallway as she moved towards the door, his head down, contemplating his shoes. Mrs Hammond patted him briefly on the head in passing, a gesture that elicited an instinctive withdrawal on the boy's part, which she either failed to notice or deliberately ignored.

'See you again soon,' she said, and Tessa wondered if it was only her imagination that made the words sound like a faint threat.

Recalling the encounter now, she felt the same sharp distaste. Jason had said little after the woman had gone, only that she was a friend of his father's. Tessa hadn't wanted to press him any further. Whatever the relationship between the two, it was nothing to do with her. The only concern she felt was for Jason, who quite obviously didn't care for this Mrs Hammond very much either.

The master of the house was not around when they got back there at six-thirty. The cup containing coffee dregs standing on the kitchen drainer suggested that he had been back at some point during the day and gone out again. There was no note, nothing to indicate when he might be returning. Tessa made supper for just the two of them, played a game of Monopoly, then advised an early night, considering the zoo trip they had planned for the following day.

'Do you think Daddy went away again?' asked Jason pensively when he was in bed.

Tessa smiled reassuringly. 'Not without letting anyone know, I'm sure. You'll see him in the morning.'

He seemed to accept that, snuggling down between the sheets with a faint sigh. 'Night, Tessa.'

'Sleep tight,' she said softly.

She was in bed herself, though not asleep when the front doorbell rang just after one o'clock. Slipping on the cotton wrap, she padded downstairs, cautiously opening the door on the chain to see Mark standing on the step.

'I forgot my house key,' he said. 'Sorry to get you up.'

If you'd come home at a decent hour you wouldn't have had to, it was on the tip of her tongue to retort, but she bit it back.

'Had a nice evening?' she enquired silkily when he was inside.

'Fine,' he acknowledged. 'I was here at five. What time did you get back?'

'Half-past six. We had tea at my parents' house, and supper here.'

'I'm not complaining.' His tone was easy. 'It was good of you to take him with you. I imagine he's asleep by now?'

'He's been asleep the last four hours or more.'

She moved past him to slide the bolts on the door, straightening and turning to find him still standing in the same position bare inches away. He was wearing a lightweight suit in dark blue, the collar of his white silk shirt loosened at the neck, tie hanging free. That was lipstick on the point, she thought. He had been with some girlfriend or other—though not this morning's visitor because she was out of town. He had been drinking, too; she could smell whisky on his breath.

'Did you drive back?' she asked, wishing he would move and let her pass.

Mockery lit the grey eyes. 'I didn't walk.'

'You could have been stopped and breathalysed!'

'In a taxi? I dropped the car off at the garage earlier for servicing.'

Tessa bit her lip, conscious of being played with. She had spoken out of genuine concern, but he couldn't be expected to understand that. 'That's all right, then. I'll get back to bed.'

He made no move to stand aside. 'You just can't stop playing the nanny, can you?' he said on the same taunting note. 'Perhaps it's time someone taught you the difference between little boys and grown men!'

Caught up in his arms, she had no time to protest. His mouth was firm and compelling, pressuring her lips apart and bringing the blood pounding into her ears. She tried to thrust him away, but he was too strong for her. He took his time releasing her, viewing her flushed face and stormy eyes with hard amusement.

'Enough said?'

'You're not funny!' she stated disgustedly. 'Just let me pass!'

'Of course.' He indicated the way with an exaggerated sweep of a hand. 'School is out, as of now.'

She was thankful when he made no immediate attempt to follow her up the stairs. Her lips were tingling, her equilibrium shot to pieces. Reaching her room, she shut the door and leaned against it, angry with herself as much as him because she couldn't deny that the kiss had stirred her. It was said that alcohol released the inner personality. True or false, that had been a different man down there tonight: one she found even more disturbing than the former version.

She wished suddenly and passionately that she had never heard of Mark Leyland and his son. Between the two of them, she was beginning to lose her grip.

CHAPTER THREE

TESSA and Jason were already at breakfast when Mark put in an appearance. If he had a bad head this morning it was entirely his own fault, thought Tessa judiciously as he took the black coffee he had poured for himself over to the breakfast-room window to stand looking out into the sunlit courtyard while he drank it.

What needled her most, she was bound to admit, was the knowledge that the kiss he had felt stirred to bestow on her had probably been as much a product of emotions aroused by some other woman as the professed desire to give her a jolt. He didn't even appear to remember it. One thing she was sure of, it wouldn't be happening again!

'What do you two have on the agenda this morning?' he asked unexpectedly, turning round into the room again. The question was directed at Tessa, but it was Jason who answered.

'We're going to the zoo at Regent's Park!'

The grey eyes held an expression Tessa couldn't fathom. 'Just the day for it. I might even come with you.'

'*Will* you, Daddy?' His son sounded ecstatic. 'Gosh, that will be great! Won't it, Tessa?'

'Great,' she echoed, and saw the firm mouth take on a familiar slant. She added coolly, 'Would you like something cooked?'

Mark shook his head. 'I'll settle for another cup of coffee and some toast, and that——'

'You can get for yourself,' she finished for him with irony. 'It was just a polite gesture, not a takeover bid.'

A sudden glint sprang in his eyes. 'Never short of the snappy answer, are you?'

'I try not to be.' She was determined not to be put down again in any way by this man. 'I believe this will be Jason's first visit to the zoo.' It was as much an accusation as a statement of fact. 'How long since you were there?'

'Around twenty-five years, I'd say.' He sounded easy enough, but to judge from the slight tautening of his lips the point had gone home. 'I imagine you're a regular yourself?'

'Not really,' she admitted, already regretting the dig at a time when he was at least making some effort towards indulging his son's needs. 'I haven't had all that many jobs around the London area. I thought we might make a day of it and stay for lunch, but if you're busy this afternoon——'

'I'm not,' he said. 'Nothing I can't shelve, at any rate. I plan on starting work tomorrow, so this may be the last day I have free for some time.'

'In that case, perhaps you might like to take Jason on your own,' she suggested, and scarcely knew whether to be pleased or otherwise when Jason himself firmly scotched that idea.

'You have to come too, Tessa!'

Mark's smile was sardonic. 'Seems you're outvoted. If the offer still stands, I'll buy that toast. Three slices should do it.'

'I'm going to find my Polaroid camera,' declared Jason happily, sliding from his seat. 'You won't go without me, will you?'

'We shan't be going at all for at least another hour,' Tessa assured him. 'It's only just gone eight-thirty.'

She busied herself with the toaster after he had left the room, self-conscious now that she was alone again with Mark. He had seated himself at the table, leaning back in the chair with legs comfortably stretched as he waited, hands thrust into the pockets of his tailored trousers.

'I owe you an apology for last night,' he proffered after a moment or two, taking her by surprise because it was the last thing she was expecting. 'Not that you didn't ask for it, with that Mary Poppins act of yours!'

'Mary Poppins would probably have turned you back into a frog,' she retorted, stung by the intimation.

'Which makes me a prince now? Gratifying!'

Meeting the grey eyes, she felt her stomach muscles contract. 'Apology accepted,' she acknowledged with what cool dignity she could muster. 'Let's just forget it, shall we?'

'Not all that easy.' The taunt was definitely back. 'I might feel bound to apologise for the approach, but that doesn't mean I didn't enjoy kissing you.'

'You're probably confusing me with someone else,' she said, recovering her poise.

'Meaning that one woman is much the same as another?' He shook his head. 'Not true.'

'You've had so much experience?'

'Enough to recognise that you're perhaps not quite as immune from human frailty as you make out.'

This conversation, Tessa decided, had gone too far. 'I'm here to look after your son,' she declared. 'Nothing else. What happened last night happened because you were inebriated enough——'

The derisive slant of his lip cut her short. 'Only you would come up with inebriated instead of plain drunk! Not that I was that, either. Perhaps just a little short on circumspection, considering.'

'Meaning that kissing the hired help is outside your normal code of ethics?' Her head was up, her eyes sparkling with an anger directed as much her own way as his for allowing herself to be rattled. 'You don't need to worry, Mr Leyland. I'm no more likely to be carried away by a momentary lapse than you are!'

'Reassuring.' He sounded unmoved by the sarcasm. 'I'd hate to give any false impressions.'

Drawing in her breath long and slow, Tessa fought to regain her composure. A change of subject was the obvious first step. 'I gather you found Mrs Hammond's note?'

There was little to be gleaned from the lean features opposite. 'I did. Lucky she caught you before you left.'

'I suppose,' Tessa returned smoothly, 'she could always have posted the message through the letterbox.'

'Always providing she was carrying paper and pen.' He took a slice of toast from the rack she pushed across to him and knifed up a pat of butter. 'Her name is Fiona, by the way. She's in property.'

Tessa glanced at him. 'Her own business?'

'Her ex-husband owns the company. Fiona runs the Grosvenor branch. She's keeping an eye open for suitable properties for me.'

'You're thinking of moving, then?'

'If I find the right place. This is far too big.'

In this location, at present-day prices, it had to be worth a fortune, she thought. Aloud she said with satire, 'I suppose it would help cover Jason's school fees.'

'It would help do a lot of things,' he responded drily. 'Do you work on the principle that constant dripping wears away stone?'

Tessa hadn't really intended starting another discussion along those lines, but it was too late to back out now. 'You're all he's got. If you send him away, he's going to feel totally rejected.'

'We've been apart almost as much as we've been together these past few years. Where's the difference?'

'There is one, although I'm not suggesting that situation was perfect either. He should have someone he can rely on to be there.'

Mark didn't lift his head. 'So take the job on permanently.'

Something inside her closed up. 'I don't do that.'

'In which case, stay uninvolved and allow me to make my own decisions. You can't have it both ways.'

He was right about that, she thought. She was already in too deep to retreat without injury, yet she couldn't bring herself to say the words that would commit her. There was too much to be considered—and not just where Jason was concerned, either.

'May I think about it?' she said after a moment or two.

'By all means.' He sounded amenable enough. 'Only not for too long. There's a place for him at my old school, but it can't be held indefinitely.'

'Which area are you going to be covering this time?' she asked by way of changing the subject. 'My mother is a fan of yours. She'd be delighted to spread the word that a new Mark Leyland is forthcoming.'

'It's going to be around this time next year before it hits the stands,' he said, 'but I'll be writing about the Greek Islands. Did you ever visit any of them?'

Tessa answered in the negative. 'I was planning on taking a holiday somewhere after my last job,' she added slyly, 'only it didn't work out that way.'

The dark head inclined. 'Your loss is our gain. With what I'm paying you, you'll be able to take an even longer holiday, if and when *this* job finishes.'

'I didn't take it just for the money,' she retorted with asperity. 'You were the one who made the offer.'

'Only because I was told I had little chance of getting anyone to take the job at short notice without extra incentive.' His shrug was philosophical. 'Needs must. I'm sure you're worth every penny.'

Protesting her lack of involvement in the arrangement was going to be a waste of time, Tessa could see. She was getting the increased rate from the agency, so she had no come-back against them, either—unless it was in accusation of unfair practice, and that would hardly stand up in the circumstances.

There was only one answer she could make, and she took it. 'Yes, I am.'

Her tone elicited a sudden glint. 'Good. I believe in getting full value.'

Jason's return with the camera came as something of a relief. For a moment there she had been tempted to tell him what he could do with his job. Except that the satisfaction of walking away from him would have been more than outweighed by the knowledge that she would be ditching Jason too.

Her actions from this point were going to be of vital importance to the child. If she accepted Mark's offer, her role would be as much that of housekeeper as nanny, although the domestic help took the greater part of the load. Work didn't frighten her, in any case; it never had. The main drawback was going to be Mark himself. What she had to decide was if she was capable of snuffing out the spark of attraction he undoubtably aroused in her and seeing him simply as the man who paid her salary, because no other way could it work. Right now, she was unsure of the answer.

The day at the zoo proved an unmitigated success. Jason was in his element, hardly able to believe that so many different species of bird and animal life could possibly be gathered in one area. The reptile house in particular fascinated him. He wouldn't mind a snake, he declared in the car on the way home. Just a small one, of course.

A reassuringly normal desire for a seven-year-old boy, Tessa reflected, wondering if Mark would allow it. Grass snakes were harmless, and easy enough to take care of. It would certainly provide a whole new source of interest.

They ate an early supper out in the courtyard as the evening was so warm, lingering over the bottle of wine Mark had insisted on opening for the two of them. Worn out by the day's excitement, Jason fell asleep playing with the fleet of model cars he had brought down from his room. Mark carried him up to his room and left Tessa to it.

Baths could wait until morning, she decided, looking down on the sleeping face. He didn't waken even when she undressed him and drew on the cotton pyjamas. Only when she pulled the cover over the wiry little body did he murmur something she couldn't catch, his thumb sliding up and into his mouth as if in comfort.

There was no sign of Mark when she went downstairs again. The table outside still needed clearing, although, with a dishwasher available, washing-up was hardly that much of a chore. Housework was no novelty to her. Many of the people she had worked for had expected that, and more, of her. While she wouldn't be put upon, she raised no objections to a little extra-curricular activity. Looking after one small boy could hardly be called a full-time job.

She found Mark stretched out on one of the wrought-iron bench seats, a cushion at his back.

'Sit down and finish your wine,' he invited. 'Mrs Broughton will do any clearing away in the morning. As of now, you're off-duty.'

'I can't leave the dishes to congeal all night,' she protested. 'It won't take more than a few minutes.'

He gave a mock sigh. 'Just no letting up with you, is there? All right, so we'll both clear them later. *Now* will you sit down?' He added drily, 'I'm not going to jump on you again, if that's what you're afraid of.'

Tessa felt her pulses quicken, and kept a taut control of her voice. 'It hadn't occurred to me that you might.'

'So prove it,' he said. 'I'm starting work in the morning. Tonight I'd appreciate the company. Is that too much to ask?'

The long summer dusk was still, heavy with fragrance from the flowers growing semi-wild in urns and troughs around the perimeter of the area. She was aware of tension, like a coiled spring inside her. She had to force herself to smile and shrug and take a seat on a nearby chair.

'That's better.' His voice carried on the evening stillness. 'You need to loosen up.'

'If you mean I take my job too seriously, that's a matter of opinion,' she responded. 'Full value for money, isn't that what you said?'

'You don't have to go over the top. Children are more resilient than you seem to think.'

'Some more than others. Jason isn't the toughie type.'

'He isn't a hothouse flower either, so stop treating him like one. You can be too protective.'

'He needs protecting,' she defended, and saw the grey eyes narrow a little.

'Who from? Me?'

Tessa refused to back down. 'In a manner of speaking. You're not over-sensitive where he's concerned.'

'Because I happen to think he'd be better off in boarding-school where he'll have companionship his own age? It didn't do me any harm.'

'It didn't teach you anything about individuality, for sure!'

'You know,' he returned after a moment, 'you're just about the most infuriating female I ever came across?'

'Strange.' She kept her own tone expressionless. 'I feel much the same way about you.'

His laugh came low. 'So we do have *something* in common!'

With his hands clasped comfortably behind his head, the white silk sweater was stretched taut across his chest, outlining the ridging of muscle just above the waistband of his trousers. Tessa swallowed on the sudden tightness in her throat.

'I thought I might take Jason to the Planetarium tomorrow,' she lied, only having just thought of it.

'While I slave over a hot typewriter!'

She glanced across at him curiously. 'You sound anything but enthusiastic.'

He laughed. 'I've yet to meet the writer who actually looks forward to sitting down in front of that first blank page. On the other hand, once I do get going, I hate to be interrupted for anything outside of emergencies.'

'Do I take that as a warning?'

'Call it a gentle hint.' There was a pause, a change of tone. 'Do you plan on spending the rest of your life looking after other people's children?'

'Not necessarily,' she acknowledged. 'But neither do I intend on setting out to find a husband simply for the sake of having some of my own.'

'You mean it would be love or nothing?'

'We've had this conversation before,' she came back, not looking at him. 'Or something very like it. The answer remains the same.'

'Love *and* respect, I believe you said. Not all that easy to achieve.' He was silent for a moment before adding reflectively, 'Diane and I married because Jason was on the way. It was a mistake.'

Tessa wondered why he was telling her. She hadn't thought him the type to offer intimate confidences to anyone.

'You said she hadn't attempted to see Jason since she left,' she ventured. 'Does that mean you haven't seen her either?'

'Only once, with lawyers present. We were divorced more than two years ago. She's married again now—a property tycoon.' His tone lightened—with deliberation, Tessa thought. 'Anyway, enough of that subject. It isn't exactly stimulating conversation. If you did decide to stay on and look after Jason for me, what kind of time-span would we be talking about?'

'A couple of years, perhaps. He'd be better equipped to deal with things by then.' She hesitated, reluctant still to commit herself, yet knowing deep down that the decision had already been made. 'As a matter of fact,' she tagged on without giving herself any further chance to consider, 'I can give you my answer right now. I've decided to accept.'

It was difficult to tell from his expression whether he was pleased or not. His regard was centred on her face. 'May I ask what changed your mind?'

'Jason did,' she claimed. 'He's a very special little boy.'

The dark head inclined, the irony only just percep-tible. 'I think so, too.' He paused, then his voice took on an added undertone. 'Supposing in the meantime you decided, after all, that you wanted a family of your own?

Or were you maybe planning on making Jason a part of it?'

Tessa made an effort to keep her voice cool and even, aware of being deliberately goaded. 'If I did start looking around for a husband, you'd be the last person I'd set my cap at.'

'Mind telling me why?'

'Not at all. You're both arrogant and insensitive—qualities I don't personally find at all appealing.'

'But you're not unaware of me as a man, any more than I am of you as a woman,' came the calm rejoinder. 'That gives the situation a certain piquancy, wouldn't you say?'

There was little use in denying something she must have made patently obvious, Tessa conceded wryly. All she could do was stand on her dignity. 'I can still rescind the decision,' she stated. 'And that kind of talk is just the thing to make me!'

'Leaving Jason in the lurch? You wouldn't do that.' He studied her, taking in the two spots of colour high on her cheekbones, the tilt of her chin. 'Most girls your age are only interested in finding a man to keep them in comfort.'

'That's a generalisation, and neither fair nor true! Plenty of girls my age put a career first.'

'Only because they failed in the other direction.'

It had to be the wine, Tessa thought, that was making her blood boil. She wanted to squash him, to wipe that sardonic little quirk from the corner of his mouth with a well-aimed riposte. 'You must be the original chauvinist!' was all she could find to fling at him, making his lips widen into genuine if fleeting amusement.

'You could be right at that. I like my women duly worshipful.'

Which hardly described Fiona Hammond, came the thought. But then, the relationship between the two was still unclear. More than just business, for certain, but how much more?

'I think it's time the table was cleared,' she said, getting to her feet. 'Does that promise to help still hold?'

He came reluctantly upright. 'Any promise I make, I stand by. Jason will verify that.'

Just that he made very few, she assumed. His mood all day had been so very different. Not that a couple of light-hearted passes meant anything, of course. It obviously amused him to get a rise out of her. The fact of his attraction for her was something she was simply going to have to learn to cope with. Jason's welfare came before anything else.

He carried the tray through to the kitchen when it was full, leaning against the table to watch her load the dishwasher.

'An efficient usage of space available,' he commented when she was finished. 'Unusual in a woman.'

'You're too fond of generalisations,' she retorted, switching on the machine. 'We're not all the same.'

'So I'm beginning to find.'

He was right there behind her as she turned, the way he had been the previous night. Except that this time the mockery was missing. Tessa steeled herself not to move as he brought his head down to find her mouth. The kiss was far from tender, pressuring open her lips and forcing response, if only in a kind of defence against the intrusion. His hands came up to cup her face, holding her so that she couldn't draw away even if she had tried. When he did finally lift his head again there was an expression in his eyes that made her heart increase its mad gallop.

'That,' he said softly, 'was for all the backchat. I'll only take so much.'

'You take a great deal *too* much,' Tessa responded, struggling to stay on top of her emotions. 'I'm in your employ, Mark. That puts this game you're playing outside the rules.'

'And me properly in my place.' He sounded anything but deflated. 'I'll bear it in mind.'

She forced herself into movement as he let go of her, desperate to get away. Her mouth was on fire, her pulses jumping around all over the place. That the kiss had meant more to her than it had to him was both obvious and depressing. No matter what his faults, she hadn't imagined him the kind of man who would take advantage of his position. If ever there had been a reason for rethinking her plans, this had to be it.

Only that still left Jason, didn't it? Surely, she thought disgustedly, she could handle a simple pass without coming apart at the seams?

Mark was watching her now with enigmatic expression, seemingly waiting for her to make the next move.

'Goodnight,' she said with emphasis, and went.

Only when she was on the way upstairs did she acknowledge the ache that lay behind the anger. No matter what Mark's reasons for kissing her, she had wanted it; she still wanted it. Great care would have to be taken to conceal those feelings from him, because she had no intention of inviting another such episode. Let him get his kicks from his usual sources.

It was a sultry night and not a particularly restful one. Up and dressed by seven, Tessa was surprised and disconcerted to find Mark already half-way through his breakfast when she got downstairs.

'I like to get in a good full day when I'm working,' he said, registering her momentary confusion. His eyes revealed little of his own inner thoughts. 'I'd say we were building up for a storm. The glass is falling fast.'

'And there goes the summer,' she agreed lightly, reaching for the coffee-pot with a resolve to treat last night the way he was doing, as something of no note. 'At least you won't have the sun as a distraction these next few days.'

Jason came in yawning. He was still in his dressing-gown, the tie-belt almost cutting him in two. Tessa resisted the urge to get up and adjust it for him, too conscious of his father's probable reaction. He's no baby, she could hear him say. Which was true enough, of course. All the same, her fingers itched.

'Mrs Broughton was supposed to iron the shirts I left out on Monday,' Mark commented after answering his son's greeting. 'You might have a word with her.'

'She's in your employ,' returned Tessa smoothly. '*You* have a word with her. She draws very sharp demarcation lines.'

There was an element of calculation in the glance he sent her way. 'Don't overstep the mark yourself. Nobody's indispensable.'

'What's indispensable?' chimed in Jason, always interested in a new word.

'It means "can't be managed without",' Tessa told him without expression. 'Like needing a hand in order to write.'

'I once saw someone on television writing with his toes,' he said, bringing a sardonic smile to his father's face as he pushed back his chair.

'On which note, I'll leave you to it. No interruptions, unless it's life or death.'

'Daddy gets very cross if anyone goes into his study at all when he's writing,' confided Jason on a somewhat dejected note after Mark had left the room. 'He doesn't have to write. He's got pots and pots of money!'

'Who told you that?' asked Tessa quietly, recognising some outside influence in the child's choice of words.

'Mrs Kiveton,' he said.

Not *such* a paragon, then, came the thought. 'Not everything worth while is done for money,' she said, then deliberately lightened her tone. 'Right, what would you like to do today?'

'The Tower of London,' he responded eagerly. 'I've only ever been there once before.'

'With your father?'

'Oh, no. He's always too busy.' It was said without resentment. 'We went from school, but that was ages ago.'

'The Tower it is, then.' Wisely, Tessa made no further comment. Jason worshipped his father. No way would she demean that image in the child's eyes. All the same, Mark Leyland had a lot to answer for—especially if it was really true that he didn't actually *need* to write for a living.

She could, she supposed, tell Jason about the change of plan—except that it would be better coming from Mark himself. Last night's concerns she could put to the back of her mind, it appeared. Writing was obviously going to be all Mark thought about for the coming few weeks. Which should have been a relief.

CHAPTER FOUR

THE rain came mid-afternoon, catching them out because the forecast had given another twenty-four hours' grace. With every taxi taken, they were forced to resort to the Tube, arriving home drenched to the skin and shivering in the swiftly lowered temperature.

'Like a pair of drowned kittens,' commented Mark, opening the study door while they still stood dripping in the hall. 'You'd better both of you take an early bath.'

'We planned on doing that,' Tessa assured him, conscious of her hair hanging in rats' tails about her face. 'Sorry if we disturbed you.'

'I've managed a fair whack for the first day,' he said. 'No sense in overdoing it. I'll make tea—unless you'd prefer something else?'

'Tea will be fine, thanks.' Jason had already gone on ahead, leaving a trail of wet footprints on the pale amber carpet. 'We'll be about half an hour,' she added, making to follow him.

'Use my bathroom,' Mark called after her. 'It will save standing around waiting.'

That made sense, Tessa was bound to acknowledge. She felt chilled to the marrow after all the sun and heat of the last week. Seeing Jason supplied with clean, dry clothing, she found some of her own and went along the landing to the master bedroom.

It was the first time she had ventured in here; there had been no cause before. Decorated in navy blue and cream, with touches of gold, it was an essentially masculine abode. Different, she assumed, from when Mark

56

had shared it with Diane—although the double bed was perhaps the same.

The bathroom lay off the far side. Spacious and beautifully equipped, it boasted a separate shower cabinet in addition to the semi-sunken bath. Tessa elected to take a shower, stepping under the warm gush of water with a sense of real luxury. There were several shampoos ranged on a shelf at the rear of the cabinet. She chose one containing its own conditioner and used it lavishly, rinsing her hair until it was squeaky-clean.

Out again, she wrapped herself in one of the thick Turkish towels, winding a smaller version about her head until she could get to her own room and find her hairbrush.

Her change of clothing she had left out in the bedroom to save them from the steam. Opening the door, she put up both hands to stop the towel about her hair from falling off, only to have the one tucked over her breasts fall down about her waist instead. She was a couple of steps into the room before she saw Mark standing in the doorway opposite with a glass in his hand, feeling her face flame as she met the grey eyes full on. Jerking instinctively backwards towards the shelter of the bathroom again, she almost tripped over the trailing end of the towel, falling against the doorjamb and very nearly losing the towel altogether.

'For heaven's sake,' he said on a curt note, 'I've seen naked breasts before!'

Tessa dropped the towel from her hair in order to pull up the other and cover herself again. She could feel the blush all over her body.

'You—gave me a shock,' she stammered. 'I didn't realise you were there.'

'I brought you some hot lemon,' he said, putting the glass down on the nearest surface with scant regard for any possible damage. 'Finest remedy I know of for warding off a chill. The tea is ready when you are.'

'Thank you.' She was making every attempt to view the situation with aplomb. No man had ever seen her naked before—not even this far. 'Ten minutes?'

He nodded and went, closing the door pointedly behind him. She had left it open herself, Tessa recalled, so she could hardly accuse him of walking in unannounced. Nothing to get worked up about, anyway, she told herself firmly. As he had said, it was hardly a novelty for him. All the same, it was going to be difficult facing him again. She just didn't have that kind of insouciance.

There was nothing in his manner to suggest he even remembered the incident when she did eventually nerve herself to go downstairs. Jason was down before her, eager to impart the day's doings to the man he saw so relatively little of and loved so very much. Listening to him chatter, Tessa thought with some satisfaction that he had emerged like a butterfly from a chrysalis this past week. For too long he had suffered neglect—emotional if not physical. Perhaps, in rearranging yesterday's schedule to indulge his son, Mark himself was beginning to recognise as much.

Jason asked to play Scrabble after supper. Rather to Tessa's surprise, Mark joined in the game, proving a formidable opponent. Holding back in order to give his son a better chance was obviously outside his scheme of things. Children, he said after the former had been despatched to bed, had to learn to compete at the highest level from the word go.

'He isn't going to find concessions made along the way,' he argued when Tessa demurred that opinion, 'so why start him off expecting it?'

'Because he's only a child, and there's plenty of time to learn about life's adversities,' she came back. 'We all merit a little indulgence at that age.'

His smile was lazy, mocking her seriousness. 'You're on your soapbox again. Can't we forget the psychology for once?'

He had lit the gas fire in the open hearth because the evening had turned so cool. Stretched out in the arm-chair, with the glow playing over his features, he had her blood singing in her ears. This was how it could be between husband and wife, came the thought: the children in bed, the two of them alone together with the whole evening ahead—to say nothing of the night. She had never entertained such notions before about any one man. She had never had reason to do so. Mark was not the kind of husband she had visualised when she had thought about it all. Arrogant and insensitive, she had called him last night. A little strong, perhaps, but close enough. He might well be able to perceive his attraction for her on a physical level, but he mustn't be allowed to guess just how deep that attraction really went.

'Penny for them,' he offered unexpectedly, jerking her out of her introspection. 'You look as if you'd lost a pound and found a penny!'

'I was thinking how cosy this is,' she improvised swiftly.

'You mean you're bored?'

'No, I don't.' She waited a moment before adding on a casual note, 'I assume that means *you* are?'

'Not necessarily. There's a lot to be said for an evening by the fire when the rain is lashing against the windows and the wind howling down the chimney.'

'The rain stopped over an hour ago,' she pointed out, 'and there isn't any wind to speak of.'

He eyed her with narrowed intent. 'Are you being deliberately pedantic?'

'Just realistic,' she denied. 'My romantic streak died a death many moons ago.'

'In twenty-four years, you haven't seen that many moons. Not that I believe it, anyway.'

'No, well, that's your privilege.' She stirred herself into motion. 'I think I'll have an early night. If the weather doesn't improve I might take Jason into town tomorrow to look at the shops.'

'He's only keen on one kind,' he said, head back against the rest. 'Try and interest him in something educational, will you? He has enough cars, trucks and what have you to stock a shop already!'

'Will do.'

She had thought him totally relaxed. The hand that came out to grasp her wrist as she made to pass his chair was as unexpected as it was perturbing.

'I want you, Tessa,' he said softly.

She had stiffened involuntarily against the strength in his fingers. Now she forced herself to stay in control of her emotions. 'Because I'm here, and female, and there's no other game to play at present?' she suggested on a brittle note. 'Too bad I'm not into the easy come, easy go kind of affair! You have a son asleep upstairs. Doesn't that mean anything to you?'

'Asleep being the operative word.' The grey eyes hadn't altered expression. 'We're neither of us children.'

'You're my employer,' she responded. 'That makes the kind of intimacy you're after inadvisable, wouldn't you say?'

'You're probably right at that, but it doesn't alter my present state of mind. Seeing you half stripped this afternoon didn't help. You have a lovely body.'

'Nothing you haven't seen before,' she reminded him tartly. 'Let go of me, please, Mark. You don't impress me one bit!'

The sudden jerk on her wrist caught her off balance. One moment she was standing there, the next she was lying across his lap looking up into the sardonic features, his arm pinning her down.

'Don't challenge me,' he advised. 'It's like a red rag to a bull!'

'An apt simile if ever I heard one!' She was too emotionally strung to heed the warning. 'Let me up!'

'Not on your life.' There was a devilish look now in his eyes. 'You're too clever by half, Nanny Cadman!'

She fought to stay aloof as he put his lips to hers, holding herself rigid. It was the unanticipated gentleness that proved her undoing. Without even thinking about it, she found her lips softening, parting, answering the slow, unhurried movement, her free arm creeping up about his neck to draw him closer still, fingers tangling in the dark hair at his nape. Right or wrong, she wanted him too. More than she had ever thought possible. The feel of him, the scent of him, the pure masculine essence of him, it was all too much to resist.

The caftan she was wearing had a zip centre-front. She didn't feel him slide it open, only the tingling touch of his hand at her breast, cupping, caressing, leaving no single nerve-ending dormant. With a sense that it was now or never, she made a supreme effort and tore her mouth free to say desperately, 'This isn't right, Mark. You know it isn't!'

For a brief moment it seemed he was going to ignore the plea. His breathing had quickened, his eyes were so dark they were almost black. Wryness suddenly touched his lips as he looked at her. Abruptly he pulled up the zip and eased her back on to her feet, then got up himself, face expressionless now. 'I think we both need a drink.'

'I—I'd rather just go,' she said as he moved towards the drinks cabinet. 'Tomorrow——'

'Sit down.' His tone brooked no refusal. 'We have to talk about it tonight, not tomorrow.'

Tessa took the chair she had recently vacated. She wasn't sure just what she felt at this moment. Her limbs were heavy, her heart like lead. It should never have happened; she should never have given it chance to happen!

'Drink that,' Mark instructed, bringing across a brandy glass. He remained standing, gazing down into the mock flames. Seen in profile against the flickering light, his face looked chiselled from stone.

'You were right the first time,' he observed dispassionately. 'What happened just now makes the whole situation untenable. I'm not making any excuses. I should have had more sense.'

Tessa swallowed with a dry throat, said huskily, 'So what do you plan on doing about it?'

'I'd have thought that was obvious.' He still didn't turn his head. 'We'll see out the summer as originally planned, but the long-term arrangement has to be out.'

It was a moment or two before she could find the necessary steadiness of voice. 'It seems unfair that Jason has to suffer because——'

'Because I couldn't keep my hands to myself?' The interruption was terse. 'That's something I'm just going to have to live with.'

It took everything she had to make herself say it. 'You're taking all the blame yourself, but I have to share it. I could have kept more of a distance between us.'

His shrug neither agreed nor disagreed with that claim. 'Too late for *post mortems*. It happened, that's all there is to it.'

'It needn't happen again,' she pleaded, fighting now for Jason's well-being. 'We——'

'It isn't going to have the chance,' he came back hardily. 'I'll make arrangements for Jason to take the entrance exam for my old school. He's bright enough. There shouldn't be any problem.'

It was obviously hopeless arguing with him, but Tessa felt bound to make at least one more attempt. 'There'll still be holidays even from boarding-school. What do you plan on doing about those?'

The shrug came again. 'I'll meet that problem when I come to it. Fiona will sort something out.'

Tessa was sure of it. She drained the brandy glass and put it down, pressing herself upright with an abruptness that hurt. 'I'm sorry,' she said. 'Goodnight—Mr Leyland.'

There was an answering irony in the inclination of his head. 'Miss Cadman.'

Upstairs, Tessa took her usual glance into Jason's room, heart contracting on sight of the small figure curled up snugly beneath the covers. In a few short weeks she would be parting from him for ever, and all because of one weak moment. In her heart of hearts she must have known Mark was going to grab her; she had even made it possible by passing so close to him. Attracted to the man she might be, but she could have coped with it. Only there was no chance now, was there? He had meant every word.

Outwardly there was little change in the general pattern over the days following. Mark spent the whole day working in the study, emerging only in time to shower and change for the evening, which he invariably spent out. After two days of having his father there at supper, Jason was crestfallen over the reversal to old habits. Scrabble was no fun, he mourned, when Daddy wasn't here to play with them.

The fact that Mark had so definitely decided to send his son to boarding-school, despite all she had said about its likely effect on him, Tessa found hard to accept, although she supposed his own childhood background had to make a difference in outlook. Perhaps she was wrong, she told herself. Perhaps Jason would take to it as a duck takes to water. Deep down she knew it unlikely. At this age, anyway. In two or three years' time it might be another story.

Mrs Broughton, the help, was a boon in more ways than the one. She was someone to talk to, to share a joke with. Much as Tessa loved her charge, a seven-year-old's conversation was necessarily somewhat limited. A genuine East Ender, the older woman was possessed of a sharp wit and an even sharper tongue when the mood took her, but she was good company.

'Why don't you bring young Jason over to our local market tomorrow?' she suggested before leaving on the Monday afternoon. 'There's always something going on for the kids during the summer. You could call in for a cuppa,' she added. 'I'm at home all day Tuesdays.'

'That sounds a very good idea,' Tessa enthused. 'I'm sure he'll love it!'

She thought it policy to at least mention where they would be going to Mark at breakfast next morning.

'Should be entertaining,' he agreed. 'Just watch out for pickpockets. The street markets are a regular venue.'

'I'll remember that,' she assured him. Jason had gone back up to his room. Uncomfortable under the grey regard, she got up and began gathering the breakfast dishes, trying to keep her movements smooth and unhurried.

'You've been here a fortnight,' he remarked, 'and you haven't taken a day off yet. Just let me know which you'd prefer and I'll organise something for Jason.'

'I'm not really all that bothered,' Tessa claimed truthfully. 'There's nowhere I particularly want to go that he can't come too.'

'Then it's time there was.'

Tessa made herself look him straight in the eye, closing off her mind to his dark appeal. 'Isn't that my affair?'

'Not when I'm employing you.' He made a sudden impatient gesture. 'We've another five weeks to get through. Are we going to do it in a sensible manner, or is the stilted approach all I can expect?'

'I'd find it difficult to go back to the way things were,' she responded after a moment.

'Leaving aside the other night, what would be different about it?'

'We can't leave aside the other night, though, can we?'

He shrugged. 'You've been kissed before, I'm sure.'

Not like that, she thought achingly. Not to leave such a far-reaching impression. How could she relax with him again when every movement of the lean, lithe body, every glance of the grey eyes, had her taut as a bowstring? Whatever the attraction she had held for him, it had obviously died a death. If she didn't want him to guess that his for her hadn't, she had to at least make some attempt at pretence. She summoned a shrug of her own.

'I suppose you're right. It wasn't important.'

His mouth widened briefly. 'A temporary aberration. Let's drink to that.'

Tessa watched him drain his coffee-cup and get up to go, swallowing on the lump in her throat. She would get over him; she *had* to get over him. If only Jason didn't have to pay for the whole silly affair!

They both thoroughly enjoyed their afternoon in the East End. Ann Broughton made them more than welcome in her spotless terrace home. Jason spent the whole hour on the floor with her Heinz-variety mongrel bitch and her pups. Seeing his face when it came time to leave, Tessa was sorely tempted to take one home, but common sense prevailed. The Kensington house was no place to bring up a puppy.

It was gone five when they eventually got back. Mark was apparently still incarcerated in the study. Tessa took a leisurely shower and got into a classically simple cream linen shirtwaister she had picked up for a song in the January sales. Downstairs again, she took a cup of tea through to the drawing-room and read a magazine for half an hour while Jason worked on the jigsaw puzzle they had begun on Sunday afternoon.

Only when she heard the study door open and close and the sound of Mark's footsteps on the stairs did she consider doing anything about supper. Whether he would be staying in for the meal now that they had ostensibly sorted out their problem was open to speculation. Gammon and pineapple with mushrooms and corn on the cob was what she had planned, for simplicity. There was plenty to go round, in any case.

Mark was wearing trousers and a casual shirt instead of a suit when he came down again, and obviously did intend to stay. He ate what was put in front of him without comment, his whole manner somehow subdued. Perhaps inspiration had run out, thought Tessa, and scarcely knew whether to be glad or sorry.

She helped Jason with the jigsaw for half an hour or so after the meal, but he was too tired from the day's activities to give it his full attention. At eight o'clock he took himself off to bed, leaving Tessa to continue fitting in the intricate pieces with a closeness of attention that failed to isolate her from consciousness of Mark's presence. When she did finally glance his way, he was gazing into the middle distance, a line drawn between the dark eyebrows.

'The book not going well?' she ventured.

'The book's going fine,' he acknowledged. 'That's not the problem.' There was a pause before he added, 'I had something of a shock earlier.'

Tessa studied him, wondering what could have happened in the relatively short time she and Jason had been away. The arrogance was missing tonight. For the first time since she had known him he appeared almost vulnerable.

'Bad news?' she hazarded.

'You could certainly call it that.' This time the pause was briefer. 'My lawyer called. Apparently Diane filed a custody suit.'

She stared at him, too stunned herself to take it in properly. 'But I don't understand,' she said at length. 'She hasn't even seen Jason in four years! How can she possibly imagine any court is going to grant her custody?'

'It's been known to happen. It depends largely on the judge's leanings.'

'But not in this case, surely? *She* left him with you. That has to show she didn't care about him.'

'She's still his mother. In the eyes of the law, that gives her certain unassailable rights.' His lips twisted. 'She can also provide him with a stable home environment. That's probably going to form the basis of her appeal.'

Tessa's breath came out on a faint sigh. Instinctively she rallied to his defence. 'A stable home environment has to include love. She can hardly claim to have felt much of that over the past four years!'

'She'll no doubt have a plausible explanation of why she felt bound to make the sacrifice at the time.' He shook his head at the look of doubt in her eyes. 'She wouldn't be bringing the suit if she didn't believe she stood a good chance of winning. Her husband can well afford to hire the best legal brains in the country to fight it for her.'

'For her? What about him?'

'He must want it, too.'

'Unless he's indulging a sudden whim.' She eyed him thoughtfully, their own differences forgotten for the moment. 'Do they have any children of their own?'

'Improbable,' he said on an unemotional note. 'We were told when Jason was born that Diane would be unable to have any more children. It didn't worry either of us too much at the time.'

'Especially as you didn't even want the one you'd got.' It was a statement, not a question, and her tone hardened a little.

His smile was wry. 'I suppose that was true, in essence.'

'And now?'

The anticipated anger failed to materialise. He looked back at her steadily. 'Did you ever hear it said that you never fully appreciate what you have until there's a danger of losing it?'

She said with intent, 'Are you sure you're not just being dog-in-the-manger about him?'

'Quite sure. My views on what's best for him may differ from yours, but that doesn't necessarily detract from the way I feel about him. I love him.' His jawline firmed. 'What's more, I intend to keep him!'

'Good!' Tessa wanted to applaud. If it took a jolt like this to bring him awake to his responsibilities, then it wasn't such a bad thing. Diane had no chance of winning her case. Of course she didn't! Jason didn't know her, didn't even remember her. How could any judge, no matter how inclined, find in her favour?

'When will the hearing be?' she asked.

'Fifteenth of September.'

'That gives you just the bare month to prepare your case.'

'What's to prepare? Until Diane stands up in court we can't even be sure what her strategy is going to be. It might be a straight appeal—then again, it might not. Whatever angle she uses, I can only tell it the way it is.'

Tessa was bound to acknowledge the truth in that. She said softly, 'You'll hardly be able to go on writing after this, though, will you?'

He lifted his shoulders. 'If there's one thing any writer has to learn from the outset, it's the ability to concentrate the mind purely on the job in hand. I'll finish the book.'

'But you don't *have* to,' she burst out. 'It isn't as if you were reliant on the income!' She broke off there, aware of his altered expression.

'You seem to know rather a lot about my financial affairs.'

'I'm sorry.' She was overcome with embarrassment. 'It was just something Jason said——'

'You always question your charges about family viability?'

'No.' Her cheeks were flaming. 'Of course not! I shouldn't have taken any notice, I know. It was just that——' She stopped again, unable to find any mitigating factor. 'I'm sorry,' she repeated.

'As a matter of fact,' he stated with the same cool intonation, 'you're quite right. I don't actually need to write for a living. My father left me well enough provided for to make work of any kind unnecessary. Any further questions?'

Miserably she shook her head. 'I spoke out of turn.'

His regard seemed to soften a fraction. 'No harm done.'

He fell silent after that. Tessa was about to suggest another cup of coffee, for want of any other comfort to offer, when he said, 'I have a proposition for you.'

He was going to ask her to stay on after all, she surmised, and she wasn't at all sure how she felt about it. If, as he said, the lack of a stable home environment was going to be the crucial point, then a mere nanny was hardly going to sway the issue. And what of her own peace of mind? How was it possible to forget a man one would be seeing every day?

'I don't really think I can be of any help,' she said slowly. 'It isn't a nanny you need.'

'I know that.' His voice was still quite level, his gaze unwavering. 'It's a wife.'

CHAPTER FIVE

IN THAT first moment Tessa could only gaze at him blankly, her mind refusing to cope with the implications. When she did find her voice, it came out as a stranger's.

'You can't be serious!'

'Never more so,' he said. 'It's the only reasonable solution.'

She made a valiant attempt to regain some control of the situation. 'I'd hardly call a proposal of marriage on those grounds reasonable. Desperate, perhaps.'

'Call it what you like.' He sounded unmoved by the criticism. 'It's for Jason.'

She said huskily, '*Only* for Jason?'

'All right, for myself too. I don't want to lose him.'

'But you planned on sending him away.'

'For his own sake. He needed companionship.'

'You could have provided some of that yourself by staying at home more.'

Grey eyes acquired a faint spark. 'A man can't devote his whole life to his children.'

'But a woman should?'

'It's inherent in the female—or it should be.'

Her laugh was lacking in humour. 'The feminists would have a field day with you!'

'I'm not interested in what the lunatic fringe thinks.' He paused, eyeing her questioningly. 'You still didn't give me an answer.'

'How can I?' She was feeling more than a little desperate herself. 'How could anyone? You're asking me to take on marriage just like another job!'

'Not quite,' he said. 'I'm not offering you a regular salary, for one thing, although I'm sure we can reach a suitable arrangement so you retain some independence. As to the rest——' for the first time he allowed himself a brief smile '—we're not exactly incompatible.'

'Wait a minute.' She was finding it difficult to breathe properly. 'Are you suggesting we should—that it wouldn't be——'

'The term you're looking for is "marriage of convenience",' he supplied. 'And no, that certainly wasn't my intention. We already proved we share the same inclinations when it comes to the physical aspect, and we don't seem to have any difficulty communicating on other levels, either. A lot of marriages start off with far greater odds against them.'

'That's hardly the point.' Tessa still couldn't make herself believe he actually meant what he was saying. 'Marriage, so far as I'm concerned, is for life. It isn't something to be entered into on the strength of a passing physical attraction!'

'Passing on whose side?' he asked. 'So far as *I'm* concerned, you're still a very desirable lady. If it's of any interest at all, I thought that the very first time I set eyes on you.'

She was startled enough to abandon her stance for a moment. 'You did?'

'Very much so.' This time the smile was genuine. 'You sat there looking so totally in command of yourself. I had an almost uncontrollable urge to shock you out of it. Would you still have taken the job, I wonder, if I'd given way to temptation?'

'That would have depended,' she said slowly, 'on what form of shock you'd actually delivered.'

He got to his feet and came over to where she sat at the jigsaw table, drawing her up to face him. His eyes held a determined light. 'Something like this.'

The kiss reached her very soul. Rejecting it was beyond her. His arms had strength, holding her close against the lean length of his body, making her aware of his hard masculinity. She went on her toes the better to answer the demand in his lips, her arms sliding about his neck, her breasts tingling to the pressure as they came up against his chest. It was the other night all over again, only more so, because tonight was no spur-of-the-moment embrace but a calculated assault on her senses. Even recognising that, she still couldn't draw back.

His voice sounded rough when he finally lifted his head again. 'You see? I could take you to bed right now, and we'd both get pleasure from it.'

Tessa made a desperate effort to regain some measure of common sense. 'That would simply be blurring the issue,' she got out. 'All right, Mark, so you know how to rouse a woman. It still isn't enough. Not for me.'

'Love and respect, you said. Leaving aside the first for obvious reasons, do I merit the second at all?'

'I'm not sure,' she admitted. 'There's a lot about you I do admire, but——'

'But a lot more that you don't?'

'Not a lot more,' she denied. 'Just—well, the way you've neglected Jason, chiefly, I suppose.'

'Which I'm trying my best to put right. Better late than never, isn't that the way it goes?' He had her face between his hands the way he had held it the night he had cornered her in the kitchen, looking down into her eyes with tiny twin flames flickering in his own. 'I need you, Tessa. We *both* need you. If you say no, you're condemning Jason to a life he's going to hate far more than he would ever have hated boarding-school.'

'It won't come to that,' she said. 'It can't!'

'Are you willing to take the risk?' he insisted. 'I thought you were concerned for him?'

'I am.' She felt torn, unable to pull her thoughts together in any rational order. 'That's blackmail, Mark!'

'If that's what it takes, then that's what I'll use.'

'What about Fiona?' she asked. 'Surely she——'

'We're not concerned with Fiona. She doesn't have any time for children.' He kissed her again, fiercely this time. 'You're going to marry me, Tessa. Say it!'

'I'm going to marry you.' The words were dragged from her against her will. 'But I don't——'

He put a finger against her lips, shaking his head emphatically. 'That's all I want to hear. We'll tell Jason in the morning.' That same finger traced the line of her mouth, the very touch making her tremor. 'We could seal the pact in time-honoured fashion. What say you?'

'I don't think so.' She was trying hard to stay aloof from the desire curling through her. 'I need time to get used to the idea.'

The fleeting expression could have been disappointment, or something else. 'Perhaps you're right. We'll save it for the honeymoon. I'll be working every available minute from now on to get as much of this book as possible written—starting as of now. Are you going to insist on a church wedding?'

'My parents will.' She still couldn't make herself believe this wasn't all some dream. 'I'd hate to upset them.'

'Then we're going to have to move fast to get the banns read, et cetera.' His face was thoughtful, as if weighing the pros and cons of the situation. 'I want the marriage an accomplished fact before the court hearing.'

He was still holding her, his hands moulding her shoulders. Tessa forced herself to move away, groping for the back of the chair from which he had so recently pulled her.

'I'll sort something out,' she said, and thought how strange her voice sounded. 'I'll have to telephone my mother in the morning.'

'Why not do it tonight?' He was watching her with an enigmatic expression. 'There's no time like the present.'

He was giving her no opportunity to change her mind, she realised. Once she had told her family the news, it would be all that more difficult to backtrack. Not that she could, anyway. Jason's whole future could depend on her staying the course.

'I'll do that,' she promised. 'Only just give me a few minutes on my own to take it all in, will you?' Her laugh was shaky. 'You move fast when you make a decision.'

'It's the only way.' One hand came out to touch her cheek, the gesture somehow more meaningful than his kisses had been. 'You might bring me in a drink after you make the call. Straight whisky, please.'

She watched him out of the room, not moving until he had closed the door. Her limbs felt as if they didn't belong to her. Sitting down in the nearest easy chair, she tried to make sense of the last twenty minutes. So short a time in which to change the direction of one's whole life. She was going to marry Mark Leyland, not because he loved her and couldn't live without her, but in order to safeguard his son from what was, after all, the child's own mother. Not that the latter merited any sympathy. She had forfeited all right to the boy a long time ago.

And how was Jason going to react to the news? she wondered. They were close, it was true, but there was a world of difference between nanny and stepmother. He might hate the whole idea. If he did, she promised herself there and then, the whole thing would be off. If she was doing it for Jason, then his was the opinion that mattered the most.

Mark was checking copy when she took through the whisky he had requested. He looked up when she put the glass down beside his elbow on the desk.

'Thanks,' he said. 'Did you ring your mother?'

'I'm leaving it until morning,' she stated firmly. 'I'll be less likely to give the game away.'

'What game?' he asked. 'Marriage is a serious matter.'

The touch of humour was a reassurance of sorts. She found herself smiling back at him, albeit with an element still of strain. 'I'll remember that.'

Unexpectedly he pushed back his chair, reaching out to draw her down on to his knee. This time when he kissed her she responded without restraint. The hand unfastening the buttons at the front of her dress had the dexterity of experience. Tessa made no move to stop him because she wanted his touch, his caress, his very expertise in matters pertaining to the female physiology. Her breath caught in her throat at the first, spine-tremoring movement of his thumb over her hardened nipple.

'Beautiful!' he murmured. With a sudden movement he bared her to the waist, bending his head to find her with teeth and tongue, his free hand sliding around her back inside her clothing, warm and smooth and knowledgeable, tracing her spinal column downwards until it met the firm swell.

'Enough,' Tessa whispered, seizing his arm at the elbow. 'No more, Mark. Please!'

'Why not?' he demanded on a gruff note, raising his head to look at her. 'You want it as much as I do.'

Perhaps even more, she thought wryly. Aloud she said with emphasis, 'You said we'd wait until the honeymoon.'

'So I did.' With some obvious reluctance he withdrew the hand, dropping a final kiss on her exposed nipple before refastening her buttons with the same ease. There was a purposefulness in the way he put her back on her feet, underlined by the slap he gave her as she made to move away. 'So don't tempt me!'

'Is that what I was doing?' she asked with forced lightness, and saw his mouth take on the old slant.

'With a vengeance. I'll look forward to a little more leeway when the time comes.' His tone altered. 'Now leave me to get on, will you?'

One thing she had proved, reflected Tessa as she went from the room: he really did feel something for her! Whether it was going to be enough remained an open question.

Upstairs in her room, she sat down in front of the dressing-table mirror and studied the face reflected there. No raving beauty, for sure, and yet Mark seemed to find her attractive enough. A tremor ran through her at the memory of his hands on her body. Making total, complete love with a man of his nature could hardly be anything other than a wonderful experience. Loving him the way she did—yes, *loving*; why hide from it any longer?—she could accept the present limitations of his own emotion in the hope and trust that time would extend it in the right direction. It would be up to her to make sure of it.

The study door was partially ajar when she got downstairs, the hum of the typewriter clearly audible. For all she knew, he had been in there all night. Daylight had brought a certain renewal of doubt. Had last night really happened, or had she dreamed it? Until she saw him again, she couldn't honestly be sure.

He didn't emerge until she knocked to tell him breakfast was ready. He was already shaved and dressed, she saw when he came through to the breakfast-room. Meeting his eyes as he took his place at the table, she felt her cheeks suddenly warm. No doubt about it, he was fully aware of the change in circumstances. It was right there in the slow widening of his lips as he let his glance drop to the region of her breasts.

Jason had been up and about for more than an hour. He had washed his hands before coming to the table, and brushed his hair into the bargain. There were times like this when, despite his colouring, he had a certain look of his father, Tessa thought, and felt her heart melt in sudden, overwhelming happiness because she wouldn't have to part from him after all.

It was Mark who broke the news. He did it quite matter-of-factly in between the cereals and the bacon. Jason looked from one to the other of them wide-eyed.

'Does that mean you'll be my mother?'

Tessa nodded, feeling the relief flood through her when his whole face broke into a beaming smile.

'When?' he demanded. 'Today?'

Mark laughed. 'Not quite *that* soon. There's a lot of arrangements to make.'

'Shall I be able to play with Kim again?' he asked Tessa.

'Of course,' she said. 'The family dog,' she added for Mark's benefit. 'He and Jason had a wonderful time of it the day we spent at my home.'

'Let's hope he takes to me the same way.' The pause was meaningful. 'Did you make that call yet?'

'Right after breakfast,' she promised. 'It's going to be quite a surprise!'

'A pleasant one, I hope. Wasn't it your mother who said you should get married?'

Tessa nodded, wondering if he remembered what else she had reported her mother as saying. A ready-made family is all very well, but what about children of your own? she could hear her asking. A little too soon to broach that particular subject. Perhaps in a year or so, when the marriage was well established.

The meal finished, Mark elected to take his coffee back to the study with him. 'Make that call,' he told Tessa on leaving. 'You can use the extension in my room, if you like. It's quieter.'

With Jason playing happily in the courtyard, she could put off the moment no longer. Mark's bed was made, the room itself neat and tidy. At the very least, he practised what he preached, she conceded.

Her father answered the call, warmly delighted to hear her voice.

'We were just this minute talking about you,' he said. 'Your mother thought you seemed a little bit depressed the last time she spoke to you.'

'Far from it,' Tessa denied. She would have preferred to break the news there and then, but her mother would never forgive her if she heard it by proxy, even via her own husband. 'Is Mom there now?' she asked. 'I have some news for you both.'

'Good news, I hope?'

She laughed. 'I think so.'

There was a moment's pause while he handed over the receiver. Her mother came on the line with intrigue in her voice.

'Hello, darling! How are you?'

'Absolutely fine,' Tessa told her. There was only one way to say it and that was straight out. 'Mom, Mark and I are going to be married.'

The explosion of sound on the other end of the line made her smile despite herself. She could hear the news being imparted to her father; sense his quieter but no less astonished response.

'Darling, that's wonderful!' came the excited exclamation. 'I had a feeling something like this was going to happen! How soon?'

Tessa took a deep breath. 'Quite soon. Within the next three weeks, in fact.'

'That *is* soon!' But she sounded happy enough about it. 'It will be St Thomas's, of course! Are you coming over, or shall I go and see Douglas for you?'

Good old Mom, thought Tessa fondly. She had the bit firmly between her teeth already. 'It might be a good idea,' she agreed. 'Mark's in the middle of a book. We'll come out at the weekend. That should still give us time to get everything sorted.'

It was Elizabeth's turn to laugh. 'Darling, you've simply no idea what goes into arranging a wedding! There'll be the reception to book, the cards to be engraved, the flowers—oh, a thousand things!'

And she would be in her element every minute of it, Tessa knew. That was why she felt no guilt over dumping the whole thing in her lap. 'Nothing too elaborate,' she pleaded, aware that it was a pretty forlorn hope. 'Mark's been through it all before, remember. I don't think he'll be too keen on a lot of fuss.'

'But it's your first time, and every bride should have a day to treasure,' came the prompt response. 'I'm sure he'll appreciate that.' Her tone briskened again. 'I'll need a list of people on his side, of course.'

'I doubt if it will amount to much. There's only a brother left in immediate family.'

'Oh, what a shame! Still, there'll no doubt be friends he'll want to invite. Naturally, Jason will be a pageboy, but what about bridesmaids? Laura had six.'

At that point Tessa had to draw the line. 'No more than two,' she stated firmly. 'And *you* can sort out family priorities on that score. It will be up to Jason whether he wants to be a pageboy or not. I'll ask him.'

'Oh?' Just for a moment her mother sounded deflated, then she rallied again. 'Oh, well, two is better than none at all. Cousin June's twin girls would look lovely in lemon with their blonde hair. I'll phone her right away.'

She would have telephoned everyone she could think of before the day was out, Tessa knew. If she hadn't been committed before, she certainly was now, because no way could she inflict that kind of disappointment on her mother, to whom marriage and family were all.

She felt exhausted when she finally put the receiver down. Considering the circumstances, a quiet, register office wedding would have been far more suitable, but she didn't have it in her to hurt the people she loved that way. It was only one day, after all. Mark could live through that.

With reluctance, he acknowledged resignedly, when she put him in the picture that evening.

'There won't be more than a dozen people I want inviting, all told,' he added. 'And if we're already so far ahead with arrangements, where would you like to go on honeymoon?'

Tessa said quickly, 'We don't have to *go* anywhere,' and saw him smile.

'Your mother would never forgive us. Somewhere exotic, I think. How about the Maldives?'

'What about Jason?' she countered, trying not to think how perfect those far-flung, unspoiled islands would be for a honeymoon.

'There is that,' he agreed. 'I don't somehow think having a seven-year-old along is going to enhance the scene.'

'He could always stay with my parents,' she suggested hesitantly.

'We'll sort something out.' He glanced at his watch, and got to his feet. 'I'm going to put in another couple of hours.' His gaze rested on her for a moment as she sat there in the window with the setting sun highlighting her hair, an odd expression in his eyes. 'Sorry to leave you alone so much, but it's perhaps as well in the long run. Don't wait up for me. I'll stick at it while the juices are flowing. Goodnight, Tessa.'

'Goodnight,' she murmured. She had wanted him to kiss her, but he had made no attempt. And what exactly had he meant by that remark? If he really wanted her badly enough to make being together a strain, then all he had to do was make the move. Her whole body ached with the need to be in his arms, to feel his lips burning her skin, his male hardness melting every last pocket of resistance. She could go to him, but it wouldn't be the same. She had to have that reassurance.

Sunday was the first day they were able to get out to Essex. Tessa envied the ease with which Mark greeted her parents. He was immediately at home.

'He's just as I expected,' confided her mother approvingly when the two of them were in the kitchen preparing the dinner she had insisted they stay for. 'A real man's man! So rare these days. Your father is very taken with him.'

'They do seem to be getting along well,' agreed Tessa, listening to the hum of voices through from the sitting-room. The excited barking from outside made her smile. 'Jason and Kim are having a great time, too!'

'Yes, aren't they?' Elizabeth Cadman gave her daughter a fond glance. 'You've made a world of difference in that child, Tessa. He was so reserved when he came before. Mark's a lucky man to have found you. There can't be all that many girls your age who would be willing to take on another woman's son. Not,' she added hastily, 'that he's only marrying you for that reason, of course. It's obvious he thinks the world of you!'

Seen through the rose-coloured spectacles of mother-love, thought Tessa wryly. Hardly Mark's fault that things were still constrained between them, though. She had had her chance to redress the balance last night and muffed it. He had caught her taking another look at the bedroom they were to share, making her jump because she hadn't heard him open the door.

'I was just studying wardrobe space,' she excused herself. 'I didn't think you'd object, considering.'

'So who's objecting? he asked easily. 'This will be your room too. You don't have to apologise for being in it.' He sent a comprehensive glance around. 'Feel free to change the decoration if you want to, of course. Something more feminine, perhaps. The firm I usually use would probably fit it in before the wedding if I made a point of it.'

'I like it the way it is,' she claimed. 'I'm not into frills and fripperies, anyway.'

His smile was slow. 'No, you're not. One of the things I like about you.'

'Only one?' She tried to make the words flippant, but doubted if she fully succeeded.

'There are others.'

He came over to where she still stood at the open wardrobe door, sliding the wood smoothly along. She quivered a little when he drew her to him, wanting his kiss so badly she could scarcely contain the need.

'Is it *so* essential we wait?' he asked softly. 'I want you now, Tessa!'

She swallowed, fighting the urgency rising in her. 'We're not alone, Mark. Jason——'

'I can always lock the door.' His hands were already untying the tailored bow at the neck of her blouse, the movement unhurried. 'Relax, darling. We're here in our own home and I want to make love to you.'

She caught hold of his hand as he slipped the top button, steeling herself to look him straight in the face. 'This isn't my home, Mark. Not yet. It just doesn't feel right—especially knowing Jason might come looking for us any moment. It's long past his bed time, for one thing.'

There was a moment when she thought he was going to be angry, then he smiled and shrugged and dropped his hand. 'I expect you're right. I'm jumping the gun again.'

'It isn't that.' She was desperate not to have misunderstanding between them. 'I do want you, Mark. You must realise that. Only——'

'Only you want it all legal and above board.' The smile was still there, if not quite reaching his eyes. 'I understand. I dare say I'd feel the same in your position. The male mind tends towards different priorities, that's all.' He shook his head as she made to speak. 'It can wait. Probably all the better for it. I'll settle for a cold shower instead.'

The humour had a definite edge to it. Tessa bit her lip as he turned away, aware that he was far from philosophical about the rebuff. She was close to calling him back, telling him she had changed her mind, but she doubted if he was in any mood to act on it. If only she had the certainty of his love. The way he felt about her he could feel about any woman.

All the same, that was something she was going to have to accept, wasn't it? Mark might want her, he definitely needed her, but he didn't, and perhaps never would, love her.

'What are you doing about your dress?' asked Elizabeth now, dragging her back to the present. 'It will have to be ready-made, of course, but it can't be left until the last minute either. And I want you to go over the guest list before I send out the invitations, too. Oh, and what about Jason's outfit now he's definitely to be a pageboy?' She paused there, laughing a little and shaking her head. 'It's all very well being in charge, but there's so much to think about!'

'I know.' Tessa was apologetic. 'Mark would have settled quite happily for the register office. Perhaps it would have been best all round, considering the short notice.'

'It most certainly would not!' came the emphatic denial. 'The very idea! It's only natural he wouldn't want to wait too long under the circumstances, but no reason not to do it properly.' There was another pause, a thoughtful change of tone. 'Speaking of ideas, couldn't you come back home for at least a couple of weeks beforehand? Jason could come with you. He'd be in his element with Kim. It would give Mark time and opportunity to sort out his own affairs too.'

'What affairs?' asked Tessa lightly. 'What you really mean is you don't think it quite the thing for me to be living in the same house right up to the wedding, isn't that it?'

'Since you mention it, it would be a lot better for you both if you didn't see quite so much of one another beforehand, yes. One needs to preserve a little distance. On the other hand, I really do need you here, Tessa. Do you think Mark would object?'

'Why not ask him?' she said, aware of being in something of a cleft stick. 'It would sound better coming from you than me.'

'All right, I will. I'm sure he'll appreciate the position.'

She put the question over coffee in the sitting-room after a meal Mark had declared was one of the best he had ever eaten. His reaction was difficult to assess.

'I can see you'd need help,' he acknowledged. 'And I can't think of any reason why not.' Briefly his eyes sought Tessa's, still not telling her anything. 'In fact, it's an excellent idea—providing you're sure Jason will be no trouble.'

The latter looked fit to burst with enthusiasm. 'I'll be able to play with Kim every day!'

'He'll be no trouble,' Elizabeth affirmed, smiling at the boy. 'Gerald will be delighted to have company on his walks when he's home, won't you, dear?'

Tessa's father nodded affably. 'It will be like old times, when the girls were little.'

'I'm not little, I'm seven and a quarter,' put in Jason with dignity, causing Gerald Cadman to hide a smile and do a hasty reshuffle.

'Sorry, old chap, just a figure of speech.'

'I'll drive you both over on Thursday,' stated Mark. His tone was agreeable enough, his whole manner lacking any hint of dissent. 'Pity we didn't think of it before.'

At the very least, it was going to remove the chance of any further disharmony between them, reflected Tessa hollowly. It was her own inner emotions that were going to be taxed to the limit.

With Jason asleep in the back of the car, she brought the subject up again on the way home.

'You're sure you won't mind being left on your own?'

'I shan't be on my own,' Mark kept his full attention on the windscreen. 'Dean will be here by then.'

'Your brother?'

'That's right. I asked him to be best man. Anyway,' he added by way of a clincher, 'your mother needs you.'

More than he did; he didn't have to say it. Tessa sat in silence for a few minutes getting to grips with that confirmation of what she had already known. When she did speak again, it was on a different topic. 'Do you still plan on selling the house?'

'As soon as everything is straightened out,' he acknowledged. 'We'll look for something in Surrey or Kent.' He paused. 'Unless you have any definite preference?'

'No.' She felt suddenly a little happier. 'None at all—apart from somewhere with a nice big garden for Jason.'

'And any others that might happen along.' His tone held a certain deliberation. 'A brother or sister would be good for him, don't you think?'

She said softly, 'Or even perhaps one of each.'

He laughed. 'Give it time!'

With any luck at all, time would make changes all the way down the line, she thought yearningly.

It was almost eleven when they finally reached the house. Mark carried the sleeping child straight upstairs.

'I'm going to turn in myself,' he said. 'Can you manage?'

'Of course.' Tessa wanted badly to kiss him, but couldn't quite find the nerve right at the moment. 'Goodnight, Mark.'

He went without a backward glance. After getting Jason out of his clothes and into pyjamas, she found

some solace in kissing *him* goodnight, although he failed
even to stir when she did it.

She took a shower before getting into a pale pink
nightdress, brushing her hair until it shone like polished
silk on the reflected image through the bathroom mirror.
She had known for the past hour what she was going to
do. All she could hope was that she was making the right
move.

CHAPTER SIX

MARK'S room was in darkness. He came up on an elbow when she slipped through the door, eyes already accustomed enough to the lack of light to see who was there.

'Something wrong with Jason?' he asked.

'No.' Her voice sounded husky. 'I thought it was time I stopped being so—stupid about everything.'

It was a moment before he responded. 'You're far from stupid,' he said softly. One hand came out to turn back the duvet at his side. 'Come on in.'

She went without further ado, sliding down into the warm cocoon of his arms and the realisation that he was wearing nothing.

'I rarely do,' he murmured, accurately assessing the cause of her sudden stillness. 'When we're married, I hope you won't either.' He drifted a questing hand up the length of her thigh, curving over her hipbone to her waist, and upwards again to find her breast. 'So lovely and smooth,' he whispered. 'Let me take this off.'

Heart thudding against her ribcage, she lifted her arms as he slid the nightdress up and over her head. Where he put it she neither knew nor cared. Every fibre of her being was alive to the feel of his naked body as he drew her close again, every sense stimulated to the point where scent and sight and sound became as one quivering nerve-end.

'I've never—done this before,' she whispered, feeling totally inadequate, and sensed his surprise.

'It can't be lack of opportunity, so it has to be choice,' he said against her hair. 'Why?'

'Because I've never wanted to this badly before,' she admitted. 'Because no man ever made me feel quite this way before.'

'Tessa——' His voice sounded suddenly thick.

She stopped his mouth the only way she knew, abandoning herself to an instinct as old as time. He was all muscle and power, his hands possessive as they explored every inch of her body, finding all the secret places, making her gasp and writhe and yet not want him to stop.

Tentatively at first, and then with growing confidence, she explored him too, taking delight in the roughness of his breathing, the tensing of muscle and sinew, the increasing passion in his kisses. A man's man, her mother had called him, but only a woman could know him this way. It had been worth waiting for—so very much worth waiting for!

There was pain when he came inside her at last, although he made it as easy as possible for her, carving a slow and gentle passage until he sensed the moment when agony gave way to ecstasy, increasing the pace until the great rolling wave of pure sensation caught her up on its crest and bore her along with him over the top of the world and into oblivion.

Coming back down to earth was like wakening from a particularly good dream. Tessa had never imagined feeling such utter contentment, such perfect gratification.

Mark was still with her, head heavy on her shoulder. She stirred a little beneath his weight, thrilling again to the newly acquired knowledge. She was truly a woman at last. And yes, she felt different. The intimacies they had shared were only a beginning, she knew that too. Tomorrow it would matter again that he didn't love her, tonight his very presence was enough.

'Sorry if I hurt you,' he murmured. 'It was unavoidable.'

'You didn't,' she denied. 'Or at least, not very much.'

'Next time will be better,' he promised.

She laughed, pressing her lips to the lean cheek. 'It couldn't possibly be!'

'Flattering, but wait and see.' He sounded amused. 'You're a very passionate lady, Tessa Cadman!'

Soon to be Leyland, she thought mistily. She couldn't wait! Humour overtook her. She hadn't waited, had she? Nor did she regret it. Their wedding night would be so much better for this preview.

'My mother would say I was a shameless hussy,' she murmured. 'Do you think I am, too?'

'Totally.' He lifted himself to kiss her on the mouth, then slid down at her side, turning her so that she lay with her back to him but snuggled close, his arm across her waist. 'But I'm glad of it,' he added, breath warm on her nape.

He was asleep before she was, his breathing deep and even. The arm grew heavy, but she didn't attempt to move it. This was the way it was going to be, she thought blissfully: the two of them together for the rest of their lives. This was one marriage that was going to work!

When she opened her eyes again it was morning. Mark's side of the bed was empty, the place where he had lain cold to the touch, as if he had been gone some time.

A glance at the bedside clock brought her sharply upright. Seven-thirty already! Jason would be up and about and wondering where she had got to. He mustn't find her here in his father's bed. It wouldn't be right. She had to get back to her own room right now before he came looking for her.

Her nightdress was where Mark had tossed it on the floor at the side of the bed. She put it on, briefly deliberated over borrowing his short silk dressing-gown, then realised that would take some explaining in itself if Jason should see her.

The landing, thank heaven, was empty. Quelling the urge to run for cover, she gained her own room, closing the door again and leaning against it for a moment. If Mark had gone down to make an early start on the book, he should at least have woken her. He surely wouldn't want Jason to become aware of their changed circumstances either? Not that she regretted anything, of course. How could she? Last night had been the most wonderful experience of her life—she wanted to shout it from the rooftops! How was she possibly going to get through two whole weeks away from Mark?

This morning the study door was closed. By pressing an ear to the thick panels she could just faintly hear the murmur of the electric typewriter. If nothing else, she could take him in some coffee, she thought.

'What are you doing, Tessa?' asked Jason curiously from the stairs behind her, and she started guiltily.

'I wasn't sure where your father was,' she confessed. 'He must have started work very early.'

'I heard him come down at half-past six,' Jason advised, descending the last three steps in a leap that took him half-way across the hall. 'I was going to get up too, but I fell asleep again.'

Luckily, Tessa reflected. If last night was to be repeated—and she hoped it was—then they would have to be circumspect in their movements. Jason was old enough to recognise a certain change in their relationship.

She saw Jason settled with his favourite Coco-Pops and milk before pouring the coffee. Her somewhat tentative tap on the study door brought no response. After a momentary hesitation, she went into the room.

'I thought you might like some coffee,' she proffered as Mark lifted his head to look at her with an abstracted expression. 'And what about something to eat?'

He cleared a space among the scattered papers at his elbow with a sweep of his hand and took the cup from her, eyes returning immediately to the page set in the typewriter itself. 'Later,' he acknowledged briefly. 'Thanks, Tessa.'

It was obvious that her presence was far from welcome. Biting her lip, Tessa left the room, closing the door behind her with a firm click. For all the indication he had given, last night might never have happened. By no means a new experience for him, of course. There had been other women in his life, apart from Diane. All the same, she would have given him credit for realising what it had meant to her. The light had faded a little from her day.

She was in the kitchen preparing a ham salad for lunch when the front doorbell rang just before ten o'clock. For a moment she was even tempted to ignore it and let Mark answer it himself, but it was beyond her to be as childishly petulant as that. The man who stood on the doorstep was enough like Mark in both colouring and bone-structure to make the relationship apparent, yet somehow quite different. Not just the age-gap alone, thought Tessa, meeting the frankly curious blue-grey eyes: it was his whole manner.

'I'm Dean,' he stated with a hint of a Canadian drawl. 'Do I take it you're my sister-in-law to be?'

Feeling more than a little awkward, Tessa held out a hand. 'Hello, Dean. I—We weren't expecting you for another week or so.'

'Change of plan.' He added pointedly, 'Do I get to come in?'

'Oh, I'm sorry!' Flustered, she stood back from the doorway. 'Of course!'

He picked up the single suitcase and moved over the threshold, casting a swift and somewhat disparaging look around. 'Same old place. That wallcovering must have been on more than ten years!'

'Quality lasts,' Tessa responded, recovering a little from the initial surprise. 'Did you have a good journey?'

'Not bad for a red-eye flight.' There was a certain speculation in the regard he brought back to her face. 'You're not what I expected.'

The opening of the study door saved Tessa from finding an answer to that observation, although she would have been interested to hear just what it was he *had* expected. Mark looked more resigned than surprised, she thought.

'Good to see you,' he said to his brother. 'Why didn't you let us know you were coming in early?'

'Last-minute decision.' Dean was somehow not as casual as he was making out. 'Is there any chance of any breakfast? I came straight on from Heathrow.'

'I'll get you something,' Tessa offered. She looked Mark's way a little diffidently. 'How about you?'

'May as well, I suppose.' The sudden smile warmed her heart. 'I just discovered I'm hungry.'

'Ten minutes,' she promised. 'You must have lots to talk about, you two. Why don't you go and sit down, and I'll call you through when it's ready?'

She made for the kitchen again with buoyant step. One smile from the man and she was ready to jump through hoops! That was what love was about though, wasn't it? One-sided or not, she wouldn't be without it.

If anything, Mark's air of resignation seemed to have deepened by the time she called the two men through to the breakfast room. Dean himself wasn't nearly as jaunty as when he had first walked through the door, although he perked up interest when Tessa put a loaded plate down in front of him.

'Not just a pretty face,' he commented. 'This is just what the doctor ordered!'

'There'll be some more luggage arriving later today,' said Mark before starting to eat. 'Dean won't be going back to Canada.'

'Oh?' Tessa looked from one to the other, scarcely knowing what else to say. 'I see,' she finished lamely. 'I'll just go and make sure the room is ready.'

Mrs Broughton was working upstairs. She clicked her tongue when told of the new addition to the household.

'Hasn't been over there a year yet,' she said. 'Wouldn't surprise me to hear he'd got the push from his job. A real charmer, that young man, when he wants to be, but he thinks the world owes him a living. Lost all his own money playing the stock markets, from what I heard, so he sponges off Mr Mark. It was him as fixed up this job in Canada. Always knew it wouldn't last.'

'Perhaps he just didn't like the country,' suggested Tessa mildly, knowing she shouldn't really be listening to all this gossip, but unable to turn a deaf ear either. 'Now that he's home, he'll be able to look around for something else.'

'Now that he's home, you'll be lucky to get rid of him at all,' was the dark prediction. 'You see if I'm right!'

Mark went back to work right after the meal, leaving Tessa to show his brother which room had been prepared for him.

'You didn't have to bother,' Dean advised easily. 'I lived here, man and boy, for enough years to know my way around. Where's Jason, by the way?'

'He was in his room,' Tessa acknowledged, wondering if the snub had been intentional or not. 'He's building a model plane.'

Dean crossed the landing to open the other door, eliciting a cry of delight from within.

'Uncle Dean!'

Tessa went slowly back downstairs, feeling suddenly and unaccountably depressed. Dean wasn't going to be here long, she consoled herself. Just until he found himself another job and somewhere to live. That such a process might take months, she resolutely put to the back of her mind. This house was big enough for all of them.

Dean did some telephoning after lunch, and announced he would be out to dinner. Renewing old contacts, he said lightly in answer to Mark's dry comment.

'Does Dean know why we're getting married?' asked Tessa as casually as she could after Jason was out of the way that evening.

'You mean the custody suit?' Mark shook his head. 'No one else knows about that yet.'

She said worriedly, 'Will Jason have to be in court?'

'Hopefully not. I'd prefer to keep him right out of it.'

'I hope so!'

The lean features wore an unreadable expression as he studied her across the few feet of firelit space between them. 'Shall you worry about me the same way when we're married?' he asked on a note that should have been bantering but somehow wasn't.

'You're adult, and capable of looking after your own interests,' she responded.

'But not Jason's?'

She sighed. 'That wasn't what I meant.'

'I know.' He said it gently. 'You're a very special kind of person, Tessa. I don't know any other who could have made the gesture you made last night.'

Was that all it had been to him—a gesture? she wondered bleakly. Yet what more could she expect? She already knew he didn't love her. At least he had the integrity not to try pretending.

'With Dean in the house, I think we're going to have to settle for what we've had,' he added with regretful intonation. 'There's no way I'm going to risk putting you in line for the kind of innuendo he's likely to come up with if he suspects we're anticipating the event. Perhaps as well you're going to Essex on Thursday. Easier to stay celibate when the temptation is removed.'

There's here and now, she wanted to say, desperate for the feel of his arms, of his lips. Make love to me *now*, Mark! Instead, she heard her own voice, calm and cool and infinitely collected. 'I'm sure we'll neither of us have time to feel too deprived.'

His lips twisted. 'I'm sure you're right. Talking of time, I'd better make use of it.'

'You're going back to work?' she asked dismally as he got to his feet.

'I want to get as much of this book done as possible before the wedding, even if I don't finish it,' he said. 'The lack of distraction these next two weeks should help.' He bent down in passing her chair to drop a light kiss on her forehead. 'Don't wait up. I'll probably be burning the midnight oil.'

She said tonelessly, 'Shall I bring you in a drink or anything later?'

He shook his head. 'If I have anything at all it will be a whisky, and the decanter in the study is more than half full. Goodnight, Tessa.'

He was gone almost before she could reply, leaving her to gaze into the fire with a feeling that the next two days were going to seem more like two years. All because Dean had elected to return, she thought with unaccustomed bitterness. She could only hope he would be gone by the time they returned from honeymoon.

In actual fact, the time went by quite quickly. She spent a great deal of it putting pre-prepared meals in the freezer for both men to help themselves from when the fancy took them. Using the preheat cycle on the microwave, they would take only minutes to prepare. Certainly, if Mark was going to be sticking at it as hard as he said he would be, then he would have little time for anything more elaborate.

Of Dean himself she saw comparatively little. He was out each evening, returning late—or early, dependent on which way one looked at it—and rising only when he smelled breakfast being prepared. As Mrs Broughton had said, he could be quite the charmer when he set himself out to be, but Tessa couldn't bring herself to relax in his company. Jason liked him well enough, despite the fact that he hadn't seen him in almost a year. Uncle Dean was fun, he declared. He told silly jokes.

Thursday morning found Jason down in the kitchen before Tessa got there herself. Washed and dressed, he had poured himself a glass of orange juice and was sitting at the table turning the pages of the daily newspaper as if he understood every word.

'I've done my packing,' he announced. 'How soon are we going?'

'Certainly not before breakfast,' Tessa answered, smiling despite herself at the eagerness. 'You don't mind leaving Daddy on his own, then?'

'Daddy won't be on his own,' said Dean, following her into the room. 'I'm here.' There was an odd expression in the grey-blue eyes meeting hers as she turned. 'Where exactly are you supposed to be going?'

'Jason and I are to stay at my parents' home until the wedding,' she told him. 'My mother needs my help with the arrangements.'

'So Mark and I have to fend for ourselves for a fortnight, do we?'

'Not quite,' she said. 'There's Mrs Broughton.'

He pulled a face, making Jason laugh. 'She doesn't brighten the place up the way you do, sister-in-law to be. And who's to prepare our victuals, I ask you?'

'You could always eat out,' she responded, stifling her initial impulse.

'That,' he said, 'unfortunately costs money, of which I'm in short supply at present.'

'So perhaps you should get a job,' she suggested, and drew a lazy smile.

'Easier said than done, sweet sister. Jobs that carry the kind of salary I need to live on are few and far between.'

'You could always lower your standards a little.'

'Not my style.' His gaze had sharpened, though his tone was still easy. 'Perhaps I should find myself a rich widow—or even a divorcee.'

She had asked for that, Tessa acknowledged wryly. Mark wouldn't thank her for taking it on herself to tell his brother a few home truths, especially with Jason looking on. 'I'm sorry,' she said. 'I had no right to tell you what you should do.'

His shrug made light of the moment. 'No hassle. You look a bit tired this morning. Guess you didn't get too much sleep last night?'

Tessa felt her colour rise and could have kicked herself. Innuendo was the right word. Mark knew his brother only too well. That the dig had no basis in fact was neither here nor there. 'Quite enough, thanks,' she said, trying to sound natural about it. 'What would you like for breakfast?'

'Whatever Mark's having, I expect.' He was still far from friendly. 'He's getting the best of both worlds with you, isn't he? A qualified children's nurse and a house-keeper rolled into one!'

Tessa made no answer to that. She had started the slanging match; she could hardly blame Dean for carrying it on. All the same, the allusion hurt. Was it so obvious that Mark didn't love her?

Jason was looking from one to the other with a faintly worried expression, obviously sensing friction, if not aware of its cause. She smiled at him reassuringly before turning back to her duties, thankful when Dean moved out of the kitchen. There was a side to his nature she hadn't suspected. Not a man to make an enemy of, for sure. So keep your nose out of other people's business, she told herself ruefully. Mark would sort him out when he was good and ready.

Breakfast was well on the way before the latter put in an appearance. 'Have you seen the morning paper?' he asked, coming into the kitchen. A grin crossed his face as Jason hurriedly folded the pages back together again. 'I can wait if you haven't finished with it.'

'I looked at all the pictures,' replied his son, taking the comment at face value. 'You can have it now, Daddy.' He added eagerly. 'Are we going right after breakfast?'

'Can't wait to see that dog again, can you?' Grey eyes sought brown, the message in them hard to define. 'It's up to Tessa.'

'I still have to pack,' she confessed. 'If we get there for lunch time, you can eat with us before coming back to town.'

'I've an appointment at three,' he said. 'It's going to be tight. Has Dean come down yet?'

'He's in the drawing-room, I think.'

'As good a place as any.'

Whatever was said between the two brothers, it was obviously not to Dean's liking. Beyond the occasional monosyllable, he ate what was put before him without speaking. Mark himself was a little tight-lipped. If he had chosen this morning to start quizzing Dean about his future plans, reflected Tessa, the latter was going to think they were ganging up on him.

Sensing the atmosphere, Jason was subdued. He only cheered up when Tessa suggested he help her pack her things. At some point she had to find the opportunity to go through his case without his seeing her, as she doubted very much if his idea of what he might need would coincide with hers.

He kept up a lively conversation all the way out to Maldon. Responding to the telephone call Tessa had made earlier, Elizabeth had lunch almost prepared when they got there at twelve. The big surprise was sister Laura, over from Upminster for the day and eager to meet the man who had claimed Tessa's hand at last. Roger, unfortunately, was out of the country at present.

Delighted as she was to see her, Tessa was unable to stifle the momentary pang as she watched Mark succumb without a struggle to Laura's vivacious personality and pretty face. Normally a chestnut-brown like her own, her sister's hair was now a dark honey-blonde, cleverly streaked. To judge from her slender, supple figure, one would never guess she had borne two children.

'I left them with Nana Willoughby,' she said when asked. 'Robert gets car-sick, and Nigel comes out in sympathy.'

'How old are they?' queried Mark.

'Four and two.' She smiled at Jason. 'A little bit young for you, I'm afraid. Robert only just started kindergarten.'

'I'm at prep school,' he told her with pride. 'I was going to go to boarding-school, but now that Tessa's going to live with us I don't have to any more. Do I, Daddy?' The last with just a trace of remaining doubt.

Mark shook his head. 'Not until you're older, at any rate.'

And always providing this claim of Diane's was given the judgement it deserved, thought Tessa, forcing herself to remember the real reason Mark had asked her to marry him. For the first time it occurred to her to wonder what his attitude would be should custody be taken from him. It was an outside chance, of course, but a chance nevertheless. For Jason's sake—and for her own—it mustn't happen!

'Darling, he's simply fabulous!' exclaimed Laura extravagantly when both men were out of earshot for the moment. 'I could fall for him myself! Anyhow, I'm sure the two of you are going to be blissfully happy. How could you fail?'

Tessa murmured some appropriate response, feeling tired and more than a little depressed. So far as everyone else was concerned, they had everything going for them. She and Mark himself were the only ones who knew the true state of affairs, and his mind was still a closed book to her.

He left before two. Accompanying him out to the car, Tessa was surprised and delighted when he drew her to him and kissed her with more than a hint of passion.

'I'm going to miss you,' he said. 'Both of you! I'll be over as soon as I can.'

'No.' With confidence restored, she could afford to make gestures. 'You can spend the next fortnight enjoying your last days of bachelorhood before settling down to full family responsibilities.'

His answering smile was faint. 'You make it sound like a life sentence. Still, if that's the way you want it——'

She didn't. She wanted him right there at her side, only she still lacked the courage to tell him so. Watching him drive away, she felt as if a major part of her was going with him.

As weddings went, Tessa's was perfect. At least, that was the opinion most appeared to hold. For Tessa herself, the ceremony seemed over in a flash. Before she knew it she was standing at Mark's side in the receiving line, welcoming their guests to a luncheon she knew she was going to be unable to swallow from sheer happiness. It was over. She was Mrs Mark Leyland. It still didn't seem real.

Mark's hand under her elbow was real enough, though. He looked, she thought mistily, magnificent, in the grey morning suit: lean and lithe as a panther. Her husband; the man she loved. Nothing could part them now. She wouldn't let it. The custody suit had been withdrawn, he had told her on the telephone only last night. Apparently Diane had recognised that under the changed circumstances her petition stood little chance of achieving success. So this marriage of theirs had been worth while already. All they had to do now was cement that relationship into a firm foundation.

Dean was joking along the line with one of the younger female guests. Natural, Tessa supposed, that Mark should ask his only brother to be best man, and yet the two of them were hardly that close. Dean resented her; she knew that now. Why, she wasn't certain. It wasn't as if she was taking anything away from him.

Fiona Hammond was shaking her mother by the hand.
Wearing a cream silk outfit instantly recognisable as
haute couture, she looked both beautiful and a little disdainful, as if she found the whole affair somewhat beneath her. She was moving smoothly along now,
murmuring a few appropriate words here and there with
that faint, bored smile pinned to her lips. Then she was
there in front of them, her eyes seeking Mark's, the smile
suddenly deepening, taking on softness—intimacy.

'Congratulations, darling!' she said. And then as an
obvious and pointed afterthought, 'You too, of course—
Tessa? What a beautiful dress! Nottingham lace, isn't
it? Such a change from all the satins and silks!'

Tessa had thought so too at the time, so why, she
wondered, did she feel reduced by Fiona's remark? Because it hadn't been meant as a compliment, she realised, catching the malice in the pale blue eyes. Dean
wasn't alone, it seemed, in resenting her. She had stolen
the man this woman had wanted for herself. So, *tough*,
she reflected, and knew that reaction had communicated
itself when she saw the red lips thin.

'Thank you,' she said demurely. 'I'm so glad you could
come. You seem to be the last arrival. Mark, perhaps
you'd like to take—Fiona, isn't it?—to meet my sister
and her husband. She'll be sitting next to Roger at lunch.'

There was a glimmer of humour in the glance he gave
her—or she hoped it was humour. 'I'll see you at table.'

They made a striking couple, she thought as the pair
of them moved away through the throng gathered in the
reception hall. Turning her head, she saw Dean watching
her from a short distance away, and summoned a bright
smile.

'Morning dress suits you,' she proffered. 'A very
handsome brother-in-law!'

'Fine feathers make fine birds,' he responded with the familiar lazy inflection that concealed so much of the inner man. 'You look the part yourself.'

Ignore him, a section of Tessa's mind advised; kick him on the shin, urged another, bringing a hastily smothered giggle to her lips. That would really make her mother's day! No one was going to be allowed to spoil this occasion. Not Dean, not Fiona, not even the devil himself! She was Mark's wife. Nothing could change that now.

Jason came pushing through the crowd to tug at her skirt. 'Tessa, I want to go to the bathroom,' he whispered urgently, 'and I don't know where it is!'

'I'll show you,' she whispered back, and took his hand. 'This way.'

'Seems there's no respite from duty for the bride,' murmured Dean *sotto voce* as they passed him. 'Are you taking him on honeymoon, too?'

This time Tessa did ignore him. He really was the limit! Jason was to stay on with her parents for the brief week that was all she and Mark could reasonably take so as not to interfere with the start of Jason's new term. Instead of the Maldives, they were spending it on Guernsey, where they would fly later this afternoon. Not that she cared where they went, just so long as she was with Mark. There would be all the time in the world for long-distance travel after they settled into the new house still to be found.

The reception went through its traditional stages. After the meal came the speeches, the toasts, the never-ending reminiscing by relatives over weddings past and gone. Fiona was one of the first to leave, coming across to say a courteous and very proper thank-you to Tessa's parents for a 'beautifully organised affair'. Tessa herself she wished good luck, the accompanying smile belying the sentiment.

Mark seemed almost relieved after she had gone. When Tessa murmured that it was time they thought about changing, he suggested she go on ahead while he had a word with another of his guests who had to get back to town.

The room in which he had spent the previous night had been retained for use in changing from wedding finery into travel wear. Opening the door, Tessa bent to pick up the envelope that had been slipped underneath. Another card, perhaps, although why it should have been brought up here instead of downstairs, she couldn't think.

Laying down her bouquet on the bed ready to be taken outside for the throwing ceremony before they got into the car, she slit the flap and drew out the single sheet of thick cream vellum.

The message was typed, easy to read, and therefore all the more devastating in effect.

> Perhaps you should ask your husband who he spent the greater part of the last two weeks with. If it weren't for Jason, you wouldn't be in any position, much less the one you're enjoying now. Make the most of it; it won't last!

CHAPTER SEVEN

FIONA, or Dean? Tessa wondered in those first numbed moments. Either one was capable, she supposed, although why the latter should feel vindictive towards her she still wasn't sure. She was taking nothing away from him by marrying his brother.

That wasn't really the question at the moment, though, was it? If Fiona Hammond was the 'who' referred to, it would explain the look shared with Mark at the reception.

Make the most of your last days of freedom, she had told him jokingly. Apparently he had taken her at her word. Fiona's lack of mothering instinct didn't detract from her appeal as a woman. There was every likelihood that Mark had planned all along to retain his interest. How amused he must have been at her own guileless approach that night—her total lack of experience. Twenty-four and still a virgin, she could hear him telling Fiona. Would you credit that?

It didn't have to be true, she told herself fiercely. He at least deserved the chance to be heard. He might deny it, but she would surely be able to tell from his eyes whether it was the truth or not?

She was ready changed into the green silk two-piece she had chosen to travel in when Mark finally arrived. Unlucky to wear green at a wedding, her mother had warned, but she had laughed at the notion. The wedding, she had said, would be over when she wore it, anyway. She didn't feel like laughing now.

'That was quick!' he exclaimed, viewing her slender figure with approval. 'That colour goes well with your hair.' His gaze came back to her face, taking on some new expression. 'How do you feel?'

This was neither the time nor the place, Tessa told herself, clamping down on the urge. 'Exhausted,' she acknowledged briefly. 'We'll need to get a move on if we're to make our flight.'

A faint line creased the space between the dark brows, swiftly erased; she could almost sense his putting her brittleness down to nervous tension. 'We'll make it,' he affirmed. 'Never fear.'

She moved to the window while he changed into the lightweight beige suit he had deemed comfortable for travelling in, looking down on the spreading green lawns with unseeing eyes. Perhaps it would be best if she simply ignored the whole thing—except that she wasn't all that sure she could rise above the suspicion. Innocent or guilty, Mark was hardly going to take the question lightly.

He made no attempt to kiss her before leaving the room, possibly because she gave him no opportunity. Family and friends were waiting on the hotel forecourt for the bridal couple to appear. Elizabeth Cadman was in tears. Of happiness, she assured them both.

Confetti was thrown as they made for the car, laughing 'goodbye's and 'good luck's filled the air. Tessa threw her bouquet without looking to see who caught it, sliding into her seat with a fixed smile and a hearty wish to be gone from sight and sound of these people who had all combined to make the day special for her. Standing with sister Laura, Jason looked a little forlorn at being left behind, although he knew it was only for a week. She waved to him as the car pulled away, too well aware that but for him there would have been no today.

It was easier to pretend to fall asleep on the way to the airport. Held up by traffic, they were late arriving, and only just made the flight by the skin of their teeth.

During the hour-long journey there was too much going on to facilitate conversation of any kind, and by the time landing formalities were completed and the car Mark had booked picked up, it was already getting dark, necessitating his full attention on the road out to the island's east coast.

Their hotel was a rambling structure that looked like a converted farmhouse from the outside and a mini French château within. They had a whole suite to themselves on the upper floor. Standing in the middle of the large and lovely sitting-room while Mark tipped the porter who had brought up their bags, Tessa wished she could conjure some enthusiasm that wasn't spurious. In a moment they were going to be alone. She could hardly keep him at arm's length now. He would expect response if he came to her. She either carried on the act, or she put the question to him without further hesitation. She still wasn't sure which it was going to be.

'Hungry?' he asked softly when the outer door had closed again.

Only for you, she might have replied had it not been for the note. 'I am rather,' she said instead. She made herself look at him. 'I hardly ate anything at lunch.'

'In that case, we'll just have a quick tidy-up and go straight down,' he said. 'The unpacking can wait.'

Whatever his thoughts—and he must be wondering why she was being so distant—he obviously wasn't prepared to make an issue of it. After they had eaten, of course, it would be a different matter. Love her or not, he was hardly going to spend his wedding night waiting for to lighten up of her own accord. He had given her joy from his lovemaking once; he would naturally expect to do it again.

They found the restaurant little more than half full. June through August were their main months, acknowledged the *maître d'*. Now they were almost into October, everything had slowed down.

'The whole place dies in winter,' said Mark when the wine waiter had been for their order. 'I came here once in February. There was only one other room taken.'

And who had he brought with him that time? Tessa wondered, then took herself to task for that piece of cynicism. The only one she was concerned with was Fiona.

It was an effort to eat, but having said she was hungry she could scarcely not do so. Even the poached salmon tasted like sawdust. Mark ate with good appetite himself, but then he always did. Men were very good at sorting out priorities in every sphere. Emotion was never allowed to intrude upon bodily necessity.

By ten o'clock, with coffee finished and brandy refused, she could put off the moment no longer. They went upstairs in the lift, walking together along the short length of corridor to their suite with both physical and metaphorical space between them. Only when they were inside with the door closed did Mark reach out and draw her to him, holding her with hands enclosing her face while he studied her.

'What are you afraid of?' he asked. 'If the first time was so good for us both, this time is going to be even better.'

'Better than with Fiona?' The words were drawn from her almost against her will. She saw his face tauten, the grey eyes turn suddenly steely. His hands were withdrawn, though he didn't move away.

'We'll leave Fiona out of it, shall we?'

'I can't.' Tessa made herself stand her ground. 'Mark, is it true you were seeing her while Jason and I were out of the way?'

His eyes had narrowed, the expression in them impossible to define with any accuracy. 'And if it is?'

She had anticipated his denial, even indignation, not this turning around of the question on her. She gazed at him helplessly for a moment before rallying her resources.

'You're admitting it?'

'Why shouldn't I?' he said. 'It's true enough.'

'How—often?'

His shrug was brief. 'I didn't bother to count.'

'I see.' Pride came to her rescue, lifting her chin and filling her eyes with scorn. 'Then I'd suggest you go right on back to her, because I'm not prepared to take turns!'

'Is that a fact?' He spoke quietly, almost gently, but there was a frightening quality to his expression. 'And supposing *I'm* not prepared to accept that?'

'You'll have to.' She was trembling, and trying her best to conceal the fact. 'I may have sold out every ideal I ever held with regard to marriage, but at least I haven't got old flames lined up on the side! I'll stay married to you for Jason's sake, only it isn't going to be the way you planned. I wouldn't let you make love to me again for a million dollars!'

'I'm not likely to be offering that much.' His tone was calculatedly cruel. 'And let's not deceive ourselves that Jason's welfare is the only reason you married me. You made darn sure of my financial status before you said yes. You even asked Jason for confirmation.'

'That's not true!' Tessa was stunned by the accusation. 'I never asked Jason anything of the kind!'

'You admitted it yourself—by accident, I'll grant you.' He studied her pale cheeks, her darkened eyes, his mouth twisting. 'Circumstantial evidence? Isn't that what I stand accused on?'

'You're saying it was innocent?'

'I'm not saying anything. I'm not even going to ask you who told you I'd been seeing Fiona. You believe what you want to believe, only don't imagine you're going to wriggle out of paying your dues.'

She stared at him, shaken to the core by the cold purpose in his voice. 'My—dues?'

'A small matter of consummation. I'm not sure the other night counts, considering we weren't actually married at the time.'

She took an involuntary step backwards away from him, one hand going up to her throat. 'You must be mad if you think——'

'Not mad,' he said. 'Just determined. Like it or not, you're my wife, and you're going to act like it!'

She refused to fight him as he swung her up from the floor, her body rigid. Kicking open the door to the bedroom, he strode across and dropped her on the bed. The soft lamplight seemed to emphasise the hardness of his features as he loomed over her, glittering his eyes. She made one desperate appeal.

'Mark, no!'

'Mark, yes!' he gritted.

She felt the tiny buttons at the neckline of her suit tear through the fabric as he yanked at them. She was frozen, unable to believe he could be doing this. Swiftly and methodically, he stripped her of her clothing. Only when she was naked did he step back to do the same for himself.

'If you carry this through,' she whispered painfully, 'I'll hate you for the rest of my life!'

'Then hate me,' he clipped. 'At least it's an honest emotion.'

He came down beside her, not on top of her, one leg coming over to thrust hers apart. She steeled herself to stay still and unresponsive as his hand began a long, slow stroking movement from ankle to knee to thigh and back again, only it was impossible to stop the treacherous stirring, the spread of heat from that central core, the tremoring need for more—for everything—as the scope of his caresses widened. It was like last time, only not like last time, because there was no real gentleness in him. He was simply demonstrating a technique gained through long practice in the art.

His lips touched her breast, the tip of his tongue describing featherlight circles round her nipple, teasing it into an aching peak. Without lifting his head, he moved on slowly, so tantalisingly slowly over her quivering flesh, nuzzling her waist, her hipbone, lingering for eternity on the fluttering skin of her belly.

Then he was kneeling between her thighs, hands sliding beneath her to lift her to him, eliciting a pleasure so exquisite she couldn't bear it. Twisting, moaning, she tried to escape those ruthless hands, but he wouldn't allow it. Only when she stopped struggling and lay panting for breath did he desist, coming down over her in full and final possession, each powerful thrust of his hips a token of his masculine supremacy.

He left her almost immediately it was over, rolling on to his back to lie motionless and silent. Turning on to her side away from him, Tessa curled instinctively into the foetal position, the back of her hand hard against her mouth. No tears; she was past all that. The marriage had been consummated, without love, without tenderness, without anything at all beyond the desire to hurt.

It was a long time before he made any move. She had begun to think he had fallen asleep when he said gruffly, 'We have to talk.'

'There's nothing else to say,' she responded without emotion. 'Just leave me alone, Mark. I can't bear you near me!'

'Too bad.' If there had been any softening at all in his attitude, it was gone now. 'It's too late to start backing out—for either of us. Sleep on it.'

She did sleep eventually, but it was long after his own breathing had indicated that happy state.

As on the previous time, the other side of the bed was empty when she opened her eyes again. Sunlight was streaming through the window, falling in a pool on the thick burgundy carpet.

The bathroom door opened as she sat up. Mark was already dressed and shaved. His eyes rested with sardonic expression on the sheet drawn defensively in front of her.

'You don't need that. I shan't be repeating the performance. Not this morning, at any rate.'

There was a hard obstruction in her throat, making speech difficult. 'Not any time,' she got out. 'A marriage licence gives you no right to walk roughshod over *my* preferences!'

'So what do you plan to do about it?' he asked. 'Take me to court?'

'If necessary.'

'That would make your parents very happy—to say nothing of what it would do to Jason. Always providing he really does matter to you, of course.'

'Yes, he does!' She caught herself up, biting her lip so hard her teeth nearly went through it. 'You're a louse, do you know that?' she spat at him.

The dark head inclined. 'I've been called worse. Are you going to stay in bed all day?'

'No,' she retorted fiercely. 'I'm going to be leaving this place as soon as I've packed!'

'We never got round to unpacking, if you recall. And you're not going anywhere.' His tone was implacable. 'We're going to spend the next week making out we're a normal married couple. That needn't put too much strain on either of us, as marriages go. We invited your parents to dinner next Saturday when they bring Jason home, and for them we're also going to appear happy and content. Marriage is for life—you said it yourself. I've been through one divorce, I don't intend going through another.'

'Pride?' she flung at him. 'Because you can't hold your women?'

Grey eyes took on a dangerous glint. 'If you value your skin, you'll keep that kind of remark to yourself. On the face of it, I'd say we probably deserve each other. So we'll make the best we can of it. You have twenty minutes before we go down to breakfast. After that we'll take the car and go sightseeing. The rest of the week——' He paused and shrugged. 'We'll just have to take it as it comes. I'll save your blushes and wait in the sitting-room,' he tagged on with satire.

Tessa stayed where she was for several moments after he had gone from the room. This morning should have been the happiest of her life to date. She felt sick with the knowledge of that loss. Yet to have kept quiet about the note would scarcely have been any better. How could any woman ignore the fact that her husband had not only been unfaithful immediately prior to the wedding, but in all probability planned to continue being so after it?

He had put his finger right on the spot in surmising her reluctance to put both Jason and her own family through the trauma even of a separation, much less a divorce. Her mother, for one, would be devastated. She had made the mistake of trusting a man she barely knew, and must pay the price. But only up to a certain limit. Whatever approaches he made from now on, she had to stay inviolate. He would get small pleasure from taking an inanimate log of wood!

Dressed in white cotton skirt and blouse, she went through to the sitting-room exactly on the twenty-minute deadline he had given her, to find him looking through the morning paper delivered to their door.

'Glad to see you take me at my word,' he commented drily. 'You look almost virginal in that outfit. Was that the idea?'

'Hardly realistic,' she responded without emotion. 'I just didn't bring anything black with me. Shall we go down?'

His smile was hard. 'Why not? Sex always did give me an appetite.'

It was like that the whole day, putting on a face for the world at large with enmity simmering just beneath the surface. When they were alone they scarcely spoke at all. Tessa had the feeling that it would take very little to break the tenuous control. Just twenty-four hours since they had exchanged their vows in church, she thought dully. It seemed a lifetime ago!

She had even less appetite for dinner that evening than the previous one. Mark watched her pick over the food on her plate without comment, but the downward curl of his lip said it all. If he had meant what he intimated this morning, he was going to be exacting the same 'dues' again tonight. Not that it should be too difficult to resist him, she told herself, because she despised him. More than she had ever despised anyone! He was a man without honour.

It being Saturday, the pocket handkerchief of a dance-floor had been cleared for action, and a quartet of musicians brought in to entertain the guests while they ate.

Tessa wanted to refuse when Mark suggested they dance while they waited for their coffee to arrive, but the expression in his eyes warned her not to try. Preserving distance between them was difficult with other couples occupying the compact floor space. He removed the difficulty by drawing her close, lip curling at her stiffness.

'Relax,' he advised. 'I'm not going to bite.'

Not yet, she thought. She could feel the hardness of his thighs against hers, the answering heat in her belly. His hands were firm at her back, allowing no retreat. With his mouth only inches from her eyes, she was vitally aware of the strength and purpose in its line. Tonight, and any time he chose, that look told her. Well, they would see who had the stronger will!

Hers was put severely to the test over those following moments. Moving one hand up under her hair as they slowly circled under the dimmed lights, he began gently caressing her nape, his middle finger drawing concentric circles that slowly extended to the region of her ear. The tremor as he ran the finger so very lightly up behind her lobe was totally uncontrollable.

'Stop that!' she hissed. 'Just cut it out, Mark!'

'Why?' His eyes were half closed, the glint only just discernible. 'That's nothing to what I'm going to do to you when I get you upstairs.' His voice was low, but no less of a threat. 'If we're going to make anything at all of this marriage of ours, I'll need to teach you how to satisfy me. Last night was just the pre-run. Tonight— well, you'll soon find out.'

'You're scaring me to death,' she mocked, only too conscious that it was true. 'Your expertise might impress Fiona, but it does little for me!'

'So I noticed.' He was openly and maliciously amused. 'You're trembling like a leaf already. Perhaps I should ask the management to turn on the central heating?'

She gave up the unequal battle with a long and weary sigh. 'Why can't we be civilised about this whole thing? I'm willing to be everything you need in a wife—apart from sleeping with you. Can't you settle for that?'

'Who said anything about sleeping?' he asked, ignoring the last. 'We've all day tomorrow for rest and recuperation. Our coffee's arrived,' he added, before she could make any answer—if there was an answer she could have made. 'Shall we go and get it while it's still hot?'

Tessa forced herself to turn slowly and walk back to the table, aware of his closeness at her back. He was doing his best to undermine her control—and succeeding too. How could she hope to keep her vow?

By remembering a certain blonde head and beautiful, disdainful face, came the answer. By imagining those silky white limbs of hers entangled with muscular brown ones. Everything Mark had done, and intended doing, with her he had done already with Fiona Hammond. If nothing else could firm her resolve, that fact certainly could!

If Mark noted any change in her expression as she met his eyes across the table, he wasn't acknowledging it. This was a man whose male pride was at stake, she thought. Nothing more than that. By morning he was going to know that one woman at least could resist his undoubted skill in arousing response. If it took everything she had, he would know that!

They went up at eleven. Mark made no attempt to touch her at all until they were in the suite. Even then it was only to move her aside with a slight pressure under her elbow before making his way across to the drinks tray left ready on a sideboard.

'Want anything?' he asked.

His shoulders looked so broad and strong in the dark grey suit, his whole body redolent of fitness and health.

Naked, he was every inch the superb male specimen: chest deep and sound, waist narrowed and taut, belly flat, ridged with muscle, loins——

She swallowed thickly, said with difficulty, 'No.'

'Then I'd suggest you take first turn in the bathroom—unless you'd rather wait and share?'

'I'd as soon share with a snake!' she forced out, and heard his laugh as she passed on through to the other room.

She was already in bed by the time he put in an appearance. Lying on her side, head turned away from the room, she listened to the unmistakable sounds as he undressed: the clink of change as he emptied his pockets on to the dressing-table fitment, the rasp of a zip; the double thud of his shoes dropped carelessly on the floor and the brushing of material against skin as he took off his trousers.

Bare moments later, he slid into the bed at her back, turning her over with a hand like iron in its purposefulness.

'Pretending to be asleep isn't going to put me off,' he stated grimly. 'This is the only way we seem able to communicate.'

Tessa had turned off the lights before getting into bed. She was grateful now that he had made no attempt to reverse the process. The moonlight shadowed his features even while it outlined the structure of his shoulders as he lifted himself over her. Closing her eyes, she forced her limbs to go limp and lifeless, allowing him full access to her whole body. He could do as he liked—anything he liked—but he wouldn't make her react. She had never been more determined about anything in her life.

It seemed an age before he finally accepted failure. An age during which every inch of her shrieked for release; in which her skin became slicked with perspiration from the sheer effort entailed in resisting his demands. When he paused to stare down at her she was almost at the end of her tether. Had he but known it, another moment or two would have finished her altogether.

'I'll say one thing for you,' he murmured roughly. 'You stick to your guns. If this is the way you want it——'

He hurt her physically as well as emotionally, but she wouldn't let him know that either. After this he might let her alone, she thought achingly when he left her at last.

CHAPTER EIGHT

THEY arrived home early evening on the Friday to find Dean entertaining a few friends in the drawing-room.

'Didn't expect you back until tomorrow,' he said, not particularly perturbed. 'We're going on to Annabel's from here. Why don't the two of you get changed and come with us?'

How on earth could he afford Annabel's? wondered Tessa as Mark made the anticipated reply. Unless he had found himself a job while they had been away. Miracles, she thought with cynicism, were not unknown. If it *was* Dean who had written that note, there was no indication in his manner. Not that it really mattered who any more. The damage was done.

'I'll make a start on dinner,' she said tonelessly as Mark started up the stairs with their suitcases. 'Any preferences?'

'I'll phone Luigi's,' he answered, not turning his head. 'Lasagne all right?'

'Fine.'

She hesitated at the foot of the stairs as he went on up. No way was she going to join Dean and co. in the drawing-room, yet neither did she feel like being alone with Mark in their bedroom just yet. He hadn't so much as touched her since Saturday night. She doubted if he ever would again.

Thinking about it now, she wondered if there might have been some other way of handling the situation. He had hurt her, yes, but this travesty of a marriage was no

121

way to live. If they could talk about it; perhaps come to some kind of understanding of each other's needs.

Useless, she reflected wryly. He had made it plain enough that his feelings for her—whatever they had been—were as dead as last week's news. They would be staying married because he refused to contemplate any other course of action, but they wouldn't be living as man and wife. Perhaps the first thing she should do was move into her old room.

Except that Dean was hardly likely not to notice such an arrangement, and he was the last person she would trust not to talk about it to anyone. If news of their estrangement reached her parents she would never forgive herself—to say nothing of Jason. Child he might be, stupid he certainly wasn't. He would know at once that all was not right.

She went to lay the table in the breakfast room instead. The last thing she felt like was eating, but she would make the effort. Tomorrow she would have dinner to prepare for the four of them. Rose-coloured spectacles or not, her mother had ears and eyes. One slip, and they might both be opened. It was going to be one hell of a weekend.

Dean's party left around eight, laughing and loud and obviously already well on the way to being the life and soul of the evening. Mark came down a few minutes later. He had changed into casual trousers and a thin roll-neck sweater, the sleeves pushed up his arms. Standing in the kitchen doorway as she tidied up some of the mess Dean had left, he reminded her of earlier days. If only, she thought longingly, they were back there now, with all this just a dream. She hadn't known when she was well off!

'From the noise that lot were making, I think we'll need to restock the drinks cabinet for tomorrow,' he remarked. 'Why don't you ring your mother in the morning and suggest they spend the night, then your father doesn't have to worry about driving home?'

'Thoughtful of you,' she responded.

He inclined his head. 'I have my moments. The food should be arriving any minute. Why in here, anyway?'

'It's easier than the dining-room,' she said.

'More intimate, too. I thought that was the last thing you wanted?'

'It is!' She said it fiercely. 'Don't start all that again, Mark.'

He drew in a harsh breath. 'What in hell's name do you expect? We just got back from the kind of honeymoon no man should be asked to stomach!'

'I didn't exactly enjoy it myself,' she flashed back. 'You made sure of that!' She broke off, spreading her hands in a gesture of defeat. 'It's no use, is it? We haven't been back an hour and already we're at each other's throats. I can't live like this, Mark. I just can't!'

'You don't have any choice.' His tone was hard. 'Like it or not, we're stuck with the arrangement. So what we're going to do is pretend. So far as the world at large is concerned, we'll have a normal marriage.'

'To save your oh, so vital male pride?' Tessa queried bitingly.

'And keep Jason out of his mother's clutches. That, if you remember, was supposed to be the point of the whole exercise.' He gave her no time to respond. 'Naturally we'll continue to share the same room, but you don't have to be afraid I'll try forcing you into anything else. You'll have an allowance of your own, so you won't have to ask me for anything.'

'And you'll have Fiona for solace, of course!'

'If you like.' He sounded suddenly weary of the whole subject. He straightened as the front doorbell was rung. 'Here's dinner.'

So that was that, thought Tessa painfully as he turned to go and answer the door. She had Mark's name, she had security, but Fiona had the rest.

Her parents arrived at six-thirty. Chattering nineteen to the dozen, Jason was full of the past week's events. Tessa's father had taken a couple of days' holiday from work and they had visited both Whipsnade and Longleat. Tessa was regaled with tales of elephants as big as houses, and monkeys that jumped all over the car.

'We're going to miss him,' her mother acknowledged after he was in bed and the four of them were enjoying a pre-dinner drink. 'Grandchildren keep one young!' She caught herself up as she realised what she had said, glancing at Mark with faint embarrassment. 'Of course, I know Jason isn't really, but——'

'I'd very much like him to think of you both that way,' came the unhurried reply. 'My parents died before he was born, and his mother's are somewhere in Australia.' His tone made light of the reference. 'Every child needs a doting grandmama. As to missing him, well, perhaps that won't be quite such a problem in a few weeks' time if we move out to Kent.'

'Moving?' Elizabeth's glance went from her son-in-law's face to that of her daughter. 'Darling, you never told me!'

'Tessa didn't know,' said Mark, still on the same easy note. Grey eyes sought brown, the expression in them a warning. 'I found a couple of places out near Sevenoaks I'd like you to look at before coming to any hard and fast decision. They're both suitable, though quite different. Perhaps tomorrow?'

'So that's what you were doing with yourself while Tessa and Jason were with us!' exclaimed Elizabeth smilingly.

Among other things, thought Tessa with cynicism. Once she and Jason were stashed away in the suburbs, he would have an even freer hand. Not that she cared. He could do as he liked.

'Jason will be thrilled,' she said.

'Both places have large gardens,' Mark agreed smoothly. 'I'll fetch the brochures, just to give you an idea.'

Elizabeth looked across at her daughter again as he went from the room. 'You did *want* to move?'

'Oh, yes.' Tessa forced brightness into her voice. 'I've said all along that London is no place to bring up a child.'

'So he planned this as a surprise! How many men would go to that amount of trouble?'

How many men would leave their wives out of all but a straight choice between two houses? Tessa wondered. Perhaps neither would appeal, in which case, what was she supposed to say? Would he be prepared to look again, or was she to be limited to this one opportunity? If she was going to be living in it, then surely she was entitled to a major share in the decision?

Mark was back within a couple of minutes, his hands full of glossy brochures. Coming over to where Tessa sat, he fanned them out across the low table in front of her. There were six or seven in all, but he picked out just two: one a lovely sprawl of a place covered in Boston ivy, the other a modern Georgian-style set in what appeared to be acres of grounds. The stiff card looked so smooth, so expensive. No prices were shown, of course. Such houses were not for people who had to worry about the size of a mortgage. In both cases, Fiona's was the agency handling the sale. But then it would be, wouldn't it?

'On the face of it,' she said, tapping the first of the two, 'this one.'

'My choice too,' he said. 'But I'd rather you saw them both before making the final decision. The others all have some major drawback.'

'You must have spent a lot of time viewing,' she murmured, and saw his lip tilt a little.

'I had expert guidance.'

Tessa got to her feet, passing both brochures across to her mother. 'It's time we made a start on dinner. Give me five minutes to serve up the vichyssoise and then come on through.'

Alone in the kitchen, she stood for a moment until she had herself in hand. Fiona had taken Mark round those houses; had stood in the place she herself should have occupied. No doubt the final choice had been the other woman's, too. How could she live in a house chosen by her husband's mistress?

The meal went smoothly enough. Mark saw to that. Plied with good wine and the knowledge that he didn't have to drive back to Essex that night, Tessa's father was so relaxed he was almost falling asleep by eleven, and was chivvied up to bed by her mother with apologies for breaking up the evening so comparatively early.

'He's been staying on at the office till eight, eight-thirty since he went back,' she said, preparing to follow him up. She laughed. 'If I didn't happen to know the auditors are due next week, I might even begin to suspect another woman!' She kissed Tessa's cheek, and then, quite naturally, did the same with Mark. 'Goodnight, darlings. It's been such a lovely evening, just the four of us!'

Dean had been out since early afternoon. Watching Mark slide the bolt on the front door, Tessa refrained from comment. Perhaps he knew something she didn't about his brother's movements. She went through to the dining-room and finished clearing the table, then loaded the dishwasher and switched it on.

Mark had gone into the study. To do what, she neither knew nor cared. Lying at his side in the double bed last night, so close and yet so distant, she had reached the conclusion that the only way to deal with this affair was to shut herself off from all deeper emotions and simply accept things the way they were. Whatever happened, Jason was not going to suffer. With regard to the new house, it was his needs that were the most important, not hers. So let his be the choice tomorrow. His and his father's. She wanted no part in it.

She was brushing her hair before the dressing-table mirror when Mark came up. In the dark trousers and silky white roll-neck sweater, he looked heart-stirringly attractive. Except that her heart was past stirring, so she could view him with detachment.

'Why didn't you mention the house before this?' she asked. 'Why bother keeping it a secret?'

'I planned on telling you during the week,' he said levelly. 'A kind of post-wedding present, if you like. There hasn't been much opportunity since we got back.'

'You could have made the opportunity,' she retorted. 'Not dropped it out that way in front of my parents. What were you trying to do—impress them with your thoughtful generosity?'

'Keep your voice down,' he advised, still without raising his own. 'They're only two doors along.'

Tessa hadn't even been aware of the increase in volume. She made a conscious effort now to keep her tone low. 'Speaking of wedding presents, you may as well return the pearls you bought me, because I shan't be wearing them.'

'That's up to you,' he said. 'So far as I'm concerned, they're yours to do as you like with.'

'In which case, you won't object if I give them to Oxfam?'

He observed her dispassionately through the mirror. 'If that's what you want. They'll probably be sold off for a fraction of their real value, which means the needy aren't going to get much out of the gesture, but by all means make it.'

A pretty ridiculous gesture, Tessa was bound to admit. There was no point in trying to get at him that way. It was like water off a duck's back!

'Money is no object to you, is it?' she said coolly. 'Perhaps I didn't make such a bad bargain after all.'

His eyes narrowed suddenly and dangerously. 'Just make sure you keep your side of it.'

'To the letter,' she assured him. 'I wouldn't hurt Jason for the world!'

'Nice to know something can reach you.'

He was stripping off the thin sweater as he spoke, lifted arms tautening the muscle across his chest. Tessa swallowed and turned her eyes away, laying down the brush to reach instead for her nightcream and smooth it into her skin with careful upward strokes. No reason to let herself go just because she had a husband who didn't care about her. On the surface she would be everything he could ask in a wife. Only the two of them would know what was missing.

As usual, he was asleep long before her. Lying there gazing at the shadowed ceiling, she envied that masculine ability to switch off. Her own thoughts refused to stop their circling. Not that going over and over it all was going to do any good.

It was around one when she heard the doorbell. Mark didn't even stir. Sliding from the bed, she reached for her wrap and slippers, and left the room without switching on a light. It could only be Dean at this hour, so what had Mark been playing at, locking the door on him?

His own fault, the former admitted airily when he was inside. He had told Mark he would be spending the night out.

'My plans went a little awry,' he tagged on as Tessa locked up again. 'The best laid, and all that.' The tone held a hint of malice. 'But then, I'm talking to the ready initiated.'

'I'm not sure what you mean,' she said without expression, turning to face him. 'If you must talk in riddles, at least wait until a decent hour.'

'I mean this marriage of yours isn't turning out quite the way *you* planned.'

From somewhere she found the control to keep an unrevealing tone of voice. 'What makes you think that?'

'I watched the two of you together this morning. I'm no idiot, Nanny, darling. I know my brother well enough to recognise a lack of—commitment, shall we call it? He should have let Jason go to Diane. That would have left him free to marry the kind of woman he really wanted.'

Her throat closed up. 'I gather you have someone in mind,' she said thickly.

He shrugged. 'Before this business with Diane cropped up, he and Fiona Hammond were well on the way to making a go of it.'

'You've been in Canada this past year. How do you know what he and Fiona were planning?'

'From the horse's mouth, you might say.'

'But she doesn't like children,' Tessa murmured, almost to herself.

'A good boarding school would have taken care of that problem.'

So it had been Fiona's suggestion in the first place. One she had no doubt imparted to Jason himself—which explained his attitude towards the woman. And Mark had been ready to go along with it. Her own feelings apart, Tessa thought, one had to be almost grateful to Diane for putting a spoke in that particular wheel.

'What difference does it make to you, anyway?' she asked dully.

'Fiona has contacts that could have been very useful to me.'

'Surely still could?'

Dean's smile was thin. 'Not while you're around.'

Tessa stared at him, her mind suddenly sharpening. '*You* wrote that note,' she accused. 'Not Fiona. You.'

If there was any shame in him at all, it was well hidden. His expression didn't alter. 'What note?'

She ignored the denial, sure now of her ground. 'If you were hoping I'd be so upset by it I'd up and leave him, you were quite wrong,' she said, taking a grip on herself. 'After all, if I only married him for his money, as you appear to be indicating, I'm hardly going to opt out over a last fling with another woman, am I?'

'*Last* fling?' The words came soft. 'You don't imagine it's over?'

Something knotted deep inside her. She fought to keep her voice on an even keel. 'It isn't important. I'm still his wife.'

Dean was looking at her as if he had never really seen her before. There was even a spark of unwilling admiration in his eyes. 'You know,' he said, 'I think I may have underestimated you, Tessa. You're quite something! Why don't you and I get to know one another a little better?'

She would have backstepped, except that there was nowhere to go. Dean pinned her up against the front door, a hand on her throat as he sought her mouth. He cursed when she bit his lip, his free hand going up to touch the spot while his eyes blazed into hers.

'That's going to cost you!' he gritted.

He was stronger than he looked, Tessa realised in the moments following. Held rigid against the door, she suffered the cruelly demanding heat of his mouth on hers, the hardness of the hand that delved inside her wrap to find her breast. There was no point in struggling because she couldn't hope to break his grip on her. All she could do was stay still and cold in the hope that his anger would burn itself out.

It took the click of a switch and sudden flood of light to jerk him away from her. Breath coming short and hard, he swung to look up at his brother at the head of the stairs. Tessa stopped herself from sinking nervelessly to the floor by sheer effort of will, one hand going up to ease her throat where he had grasped it, her mind still too confused to think straight.

'Caught in the act, I'm afraid,' Dean exclaimed, sounding suitably rueful about it. 'I guess you had to find out sooner or later.'

Tessa found her voice again, albeit hoarsely. 'What are you talking about? Mark, I——'

'Save it.' The tone was icily controlled, his whole stance indicative of leashed violence. 'Dean, I want you out of this house first thing in the morning. Where you go, what you do, is your own affair. From now on we don't have anything to say to each other. Understood?'

'Couldn't be more clear, old boy.' The accents were exaggerated. 'Do I get to come upstairs without being knocked down again?'

The taller man moved to create a free passage. 'Just make it quick.'

Dean obeyed that injunction. Only when he was safely past his brother did he turn his head to look back over the gallery rail to where Tessa still stood frozen, his mouth taking on a slant.

'Short but sweet, sister mine. I shan't forget you!'

Mark waited until the bedroom door had closed behind him before making any further move. Watching him descend the stairs towards her, Tessa thought of and rejected a dozen ways of denying the implications of Dean's parting shot. It was her word against his. Judging from the expression on Mark's face, denial of any kind was not going to be believed.

'The study,' he ordered. 'We're least likely to waken anyone else from there.'

She preceded him into the room. Despite the warmth of the house, she felt chilled through. He switched on just one of the lamps and went to pour himself a whisky, turning back, glass in hand, to view her with open contempt. He was wearing his silk robe over the pyjama bottoms he had elected to wear this past week, his feet pushed into leather slippers. Tall and dark and dangerous, she thought with a sudden shiver.

'I always knew you had hidden depths,' he stated with a clipped quietness far more unnerving than if he had ranted and raved. 'What I didn't appreciate was just how devious a mind you really have! You don't give a damn about Jason! He was just a means to an end—the same way I am.'

'That isn't true.' Tessa was clutching at the remnants of self-control, when all her instincts prompted an equally scathing retaliation. 'I don't have anything to hide, Mark. If you believe what Dean was trying to make you believe, then you're a fool!'

'Is that right?' His lips were thin. 'I didn't see you doing much struggling.'

'Struggling would only have incited him to greater efforts. You, of all people, should be able to appreciate that!' She ignored the sound of his teeth coming together, too incensed herself now to heed any warning signals. 'He wants to break us up. Can't you see that?'

'Why should he want to break us up?' The question was silky.

'Because you married me instead of Fiona, and I can't give him the help she could.'

Grey eyes narrowed. 'What kind of help?'

'Contacts. She has contacts who could be of help to him in finding a job. If you hadn't told him the real reason you married me, he wouldn't have had any excuse to go this far.'

'I didn't tell him.'

'Then perhaps Fiona did. The note made it clear enough that he knew. If you'd only——' Her voice tailed off at the look on his face.

'What note?' he demanded.

Too late now for regrets, she reflected wearily. Let it all come out! 'I found it pushed under the door when I went up to change after the reception.'

'You still have it?'

'Yes,' she admitted. 'It's in my jewellery case.'

He put down the glass with deliberation. 'I want to see it.'

'Down here?'

'No,' he said, 'we'll go upstairs.'

He was right behind her the whole way to their room. His bedside lamp had been left on, a solitary pool of warmth in the shadowed dimness. Without further prompting, Tessa went to take the suede and leather case from a drawer and extract the folded paper. She had read it enough times to know every word by heart. Watching Mark's face as he scanned them himself, she felt sick and tired of the whole sorry mess.

When he looked up again it was without visible reaction. 'You're saying Dean wrote this?'

'It seems like it.' She made a small resigned gesture. 'It was only the truth, when all's said and done. You admitted it yourself.'

'Which would appear to put us on a par when it comes to moral integrity.' The glitter in his eyes went beyond anger. 'You can stop playing the injured party. We both knew exactly what we were doing. As to continuing this farce——' He paused, the muscle along his jawline contracting. 'I'm putting a stop to it here and now. And I don't much care whether that meets with your approval or not.'

'My parents are just along the corridor,' she reminded him, refusing to be intimidated by the threat implicit in that statement. 'They think you're the bee's knees. You wouldn't want to disillusion them, would you?'

'So what are you going to do—start screaming?' he countered. 'Refusing your husband his marital privileges little more than a week after the wedding is hardly likely to enhance your own image in their eyes.' He took off the silk robe and tossed it down on the chair nearby, then dropped his pyjama trousers and kicked them to one side, his eyes never leaving her face. 'We're going to make love, the way man and wife should.'

A pulse was throbbing at the base of her throat, the blood pounding in her ears. She made no move as he pulled open the tie belt of her wrap and slid it from her shoulders, nor when he took the thin straps of her nightdress and drew them down her arms until that garment too fell to the floor. His hands followed the passage of his eyes, cupping each breast, tracing each curve, fluttering her skin beneath his fingers. Then he was lifting her to him, holding her easily, firmly, his lips brooking no evasion.

Lost, came the thought, as wave after wave of sensation swept through her, then she was kissing him back, everything else forgotten but this one overwhelming emotion.

It was difficult enough to face herself in the mirror next morning, much less her parents at the breakfast-table. Not that they seemed to notice anything amiss.

'It's been a lovely break!' her mother exclaimed warmly on leaving. 'I can't tell you how good it is to see you both so obviously suited! Don't leave it too long before coming out to see us, will you?'

Tessa murmured an automatic response, conscious of Mark's presence. He had been gone from the bedroom when she woke this morning, and was talking with her father in the drawing-room when she got down. On the odd occasions when their eyes had happened to meet, there had been no particular reaction in his. Last night was last night, she had gathered, this morning another matter. Except that for her there could be no going back to yesterday's situation. If he really and truly believed her guilty of encouraging Dean's advances, there was little she could do to convince him otherwise, but at least the dreadful deadlock was broken. Physical contact was better than nothing at all. She had learned that much this last week.

Dean himself must have left early. His room had been cleared of all but a few obviously unimportant items, his key left on the hall table. Tessa hated to think of two brothers estranged, yet Dean deserved no better. Not that Mark was faultless, of course. There was still the matter of Fiona's place in his life to be resolved.

'I thought we might go out to Sevenoaks after lunch,' the subject of her thoughts suggested as she turned back into the house after the car vanished around the far corner. 'I'll phone the vendors and make arrangements to view.'

'I'll have Jason ready,' she said, and hesitated before tagging on slowly, 'Mark, we have to talk things through some time.'

His eyes were unrevealing. 'So far as I'm concerned,' he said steadily, 'there's nothing to talk about. We make the best of what we do have from this point on, that's all.'

Did that include giving up all interest in Fiona Hammond? she wondered, but couldn't bring herself to put the question.

'I'll go along with that,' she said. She even managed a smile. 'I'd better see about lunch.'

'We'll eat out.' There was a sudden, unwonted brusqueness to his voice. 'And you can start looking for a new housekeeper, too.'

'My cooking not good enough?' asked Tessa with a sharpness of her own, but he was already turning away.

'Your job is looking after Jason,' he said over a shoulder. 'I'm going to make those calls.'

Jason was due back in school come Tuesday, she reflected, moving slowly after him. With Mrs Broughton to take care of the heavier work, what possible need was there for a housekeeper? Different, perhaps, if she fulfilled the purpose Mark had spoken of that night coming back from her parents'. A baby would give them both something to hold to. For all she knew, she might even be pregnant already—a thought which elicited a sudden frisson deep down.

CHAPTER NINE

WITH its half-timbered façades, steep gables and lovely old church, Sevenoaks had long been one of Tessa's favourite small towns. The neo-Georgian house lay some half-mile out to the east, fronted by high brick walls and double iron gates and set within immaculate gardens. There was even a hard court off to the rear.

The Fosters, who owned the place, were a couple in their early fifties who made no effort at all to extend a welcome. Trailing along in the woman's wake as she showed them around, Tessa tried to conjure enthusiasm for the undoubted advantages of a modern, clean-lined interior, while privately thinking that the house lacked any hint of individuality or character.

Mark brought the session to a close with a promise to let them know the decision by the following day. He waited until they were in the car again and heading for their next port of call before saying levelly, 'I rather gathered you didn't care for it?'

'Not very much,' Tessa acknowledged, forgetting yesterday's vow. 'It's almost too perfect!'

He gave her a quizzical glance. 'I thought that was what women liked—the perfect home?'

'Home being the operative word. It would be like living in a set piece!' She caught herself up, aware that it had been one of only two choices. 'Sorry if that sounds too unequivocal. It isn't my opinion that counts the most.'

'I didn't like it there either,' announced Jason from the rear. 'Mrs Foster thought I was going to break something all the time!'

'The Fosters wouldn't be living there any more,' observed his father drily, 'but I take the point. Let's hope Rylands meets with more approval, or we're going to be back to square one.'

Not with Fiona's assistance this time though, thought Tessa. She would make sure of that.

From the moment they drew up in front of the lovely old house that was Rylands, she knew there was going to be no need for any further searching. Windows glinting in the sunlight, ivy rustling in the breeze, it looked, sounded and felt like a home. The woman who came to the door somehow suited the place, too. Sixtyish, with frankly greying though beautifully groomed hair and a bone-structure that defied time, she was dressed in a disreputable pair of jeans and an equally old checked shirt, her smile totally unabashed.

'I was in the garden,' she said, inviting the three of them in. 'It's like painting the Forth Bridge just trying to keep the weeds from taking over!' To Jason she added, 'How about you and I having a glass of lemonade while your Mummy and Daddy have a look round on their own? I make it myself, not that fizzy rubbish you buy in the supermarkets.'

Jason looked interested. 'I'd like some, please,' he said.

Mrs Pierce nodded pleasantly to Tessa. 'Just wander around as the fancy takes you. There's no hurry. I'll make us some tea when you're through. It's warm enough still to sit out on the terrace.'

The tour was almost superfluous, because Tessa had already set her heart on living in this house. Oak-beamed, the ground-floor rooms were both spacious and well laid out. In addition to the lovely sitting-room with its inglenook fireplace and window-seats, there was a dining-room, a study, a huge family-type kitchen complete with

Aga stove, and a further room off it that opened directly on to the terrace via a whole wall of folding glass doors.

Upstairs were five large bedrooms, two bathrooms, and an attic that ran the full length of the house and had tiny windows peeping out below the eaves.

'Jason would love it up here!' Tessa exclaimed, imagining the space fitted out as a proper play area, perhaps with a tennis-table at one end. 'Rainy days would be no problem.'

'I was wrong about one thing last night,' said Mark unexpectedly, watching her face as she spoke. 'You *do* care about him.'

'You were wrong about a lot of things,' she responded. 'Including your brother—at least as far as I'm concerned.' She held his gaze, willing him to believe her. 'I should have put that note in the rubbish bin where it belonged!'

'And spent the whole of our honeymoon bottling it all up?' The smile failed to reach his eyes. 'Better to have things out in the open so we both know how we stand. We're starting off with no illusions about each other. That's an improvement on most. Given the right incentives, we might even end up falling in love!'

Some time, Tessa thought dully, the pain would go away. Her answer was amazingly steady. 'Stranger things have happened.'

Mrs Pierce had tea all ready on the terrace when they eventually got outside.

'I timed that just right,' she said comfortably. 'Jason and I have been looking round the garden. I think he approves.'

'It's scrummy!' he exclaimed, small face alight with enthusiasm. 'There's a tree-house and everything!'

'My husband built it for our grandson before they moved up north,' explained their hostess. 'I lost him

earlier this year, which is why I'm selling the house. It
should have a family in it.'

'I'm sorry about your husband,' said Tessa with sin-
cerity, and received a smiling shake of the greying head.

'We had forty-two wonderful years together—thirty
of them right here. It's a very special house, and I think
you'd suit it. Not,' she added quickly, 'that I'm trying
to push you. I'm moving to a granny flat at my daughter's new house, so time isn't crucial.'

Mark's tone was decisive. 'I'll contact your agents
tomorrow with a formal offer.'

'Oh, I'm so glad!' She really sounded it. 'I haven't
liked any of the other people who've been.' She smiled
again at him. 'I must confess, I thought initially that
the young woman you came with before was your wife.
I'm glad she wasn't. Not at all the kind of person I'd
like to see living in my old home.'

'She prefers the more up-to-date places,' he responded without particular inflection.

Tessa could well imagine. The Fiona Hammonds of
the world would never be found on their hands and knees
grubbing out weeds. Mark would be seeing her again;
he could hardly avoid it if he was to set the wheels in
motion. Her pleasure and delight in the house remained,
but her heart was heavy. Would the day ever come when
she could put her trust in him again?

Number sixteen Ranleigh Gardens went on the market
three days later. With Jason back in school on Tuesday,
Tessa busied herself making sure the whole house was
immaculate, to the extent that Mrs Broughton complained she had left her almost nothing to do when she
came in on Wednesday. The latter would not be staying
on to work for the new owners, whoever they turned out

to be, as she had too many other commitments already, she had declared.

Fiona herself accompanied the first of the interested parties to view the house. An Arab gentleman with a retinue of followers, he expressed no immediate opinion either way, leaving as he had come in a stretched Mercedes.

'There'll be an offer,' stated Fiona with the confidence of long experience, accepting the gin and tonic Mark had poured for her. 'These people are buying up central London properties at a rate of knots! Not that you can't afford to wait for the right price,' she added smoothly. 'Better even in some ways if the house could be viewed empty. Mrs Pierce is planning to move out herself within a couple of weeks, so providing your solicitors work equally fast, you could be in by the end of the month. Of course, you'll probably want to strip the place first.'

'There's nothing needs changing,' said Tessa swiftly before Mark could answer. 'We're happy with it just the way it is!'

'I wouldn't go quite as far as that,' he responded, pleasantly enough. 'Mrs Pierce said herself that most of the rooms were more than ready for redecorating. I'll send someone over to take a look.'

I, not we, she noted. Judging from the malice in the pale blue eyes, Fiona had noted it too. Perhaps the other woman had known nothing of the note Dean had written, but she would have approved the action. There was nothing surer than that. She, Tessa, had robbed her of the role of Mark's wife. Friendly on the surface she might appear; underneath the dislike fairly crackled.

'I could tackle any painting that needs doing myself, if it comes to that,' she said on a stubborn note, and

drew amused laughs from both quarters—or would derision be nearer the mark?

'You'll have enough to see to without that,' Mark observed, the smile still flicking at the corners of his mouth.
'Not all the furniture we have here is going to suit
Rylands. I'll leave it to you decide what we take and
what we'll need.'

'A free hand?' Fiona's tone was a subtle dig. 'How
many women could resist that offer? Don't be afraid to
ask for advice, darling. Mistakes can be so expensive!'

'I doubt if Tessa will be making any,' said Mark easily,
and she could have kissed him for it. Then he spoiled it
by adding, 'Rylands isn't a showplace, anyway, so it
hardly matters.'

Fiona shook her perfectly coiffured head. 'I can't imagine what you see in it. The Fosters' place now, that
was superb!'

'Jason hated it.' Tessa had had enough. Putting down
her glass, she rose to her feet. 'Excuse me, I have to see
Mrs Broughton before she leaves.'

'Mark, you shouldn't allow yourself to be pressured
by a child's likes or dislikes,' she heard Fiona saying as
she left the room, which set her teeth even further on
edge. The woman had the perfect excuse for coming to
the house now, whether Mark actually invited her or not.
The sooner they left town, the sooner they could start
to make something of this marriage of theirs. Rylands
had known many happy families. If warm old brick and
mortar could exert an influence, then they were half-
way there.

Mark came to find her some time later. 'I've one or
two things to take care of in town,' he said. 'Don't bother
about lunch, I'll get something out.'

Fiona was driving her own car, Tessa knew, but that
didn't mean they were going their separate ways. 'Shall

you be through in time to collect Jason from school?' she asked expressionlessly, and saw his eyes narrow a fraction.

'Considering you don't have any transport available, I'd hardly be leaving him to stew.'

'I could always call a taxi.'

'I said there's no need. I'll be there.' He paused in the kitchen doorway. 'By the way, I've made an appointment to take him for interview with his new headmaster-to-be Friday week. You might advise Miss Perriman he'll be leaving at lunch time that day.'

'You really do think of everything.' Tessa made no effort to keep the sarcasm from her voice. 'Are those my full orders for the day, or was there something else?'

'Don't needle me,' he warned. 'I'm in no mood for it. Just do as I ask, will you?'

Or else what? she wondered wearily. Jealousy was a soul-destroying emotion. Right now she almost didn't care *what* he and Fiona got up to.

The realisation that she was expected to accompany Mark and Jason to the interview the following week came as a not wholly welcome surprise.

'They like to see both parents,' Mark advised in the car. 'To do with environmental assessment, I imagine. Mr Lomas already knows our situation.'

'So he'll be prepared to make allowances for my possible shortcomings as a prospective mother?' suggested Tessa blandly, and sensed rather than saw his frown.

'Don't jump the gun. You're not on trial.'

Jason was, though, she thought, glancing round to smile a reassurance at the small, silent figure on the back seat. The only comfort was in the knowledge that once the move was completed he would be infinitely better off than he was now. They could have a wonderful time together this coming winter with the whole huge, tree-laden garden as an adventure playground. Just a couple of kids together, with Mark the axle around which both their lives revolved. If only she could be sure it was all going to last.

The interview turned out to be quite different from her anticipation. Mr Lomas was a man in his middle forties, quiet and kindly, although by no means without authority. A little shy and overawed at first, Jason was soon put at his ease, responding with creditable brightness to the few well-judged questions put to him.

'We'll look forward to seeing him in a few weeks' time,' said the headmaster after dispatching the boy with an older pupil for a quick tour of the school environs. 'A pity he had to miss the beginning of the new term, but I see no difficulty in placing him.' His glance rested approvingly on Tessa. 'You have an excellent relationship with your stepson, Mrs Leyland. Obviously your training must have helped a great deal.'

'Plus the fact that he's a very loving child,' she returned levelly. 'He made it easy for me.'

'Yes, well, it isn't all that often as quick an adjustment.' His smile was charming. 'Would you like to pour tea?'

'You made quite an impression,' commented Mark later, when they were on the way home again. 'A stable influence, if ever he saw one!'

Wasn't that what he had married her for? she thought with familiar bitterness, registering the irony. A mother for Jason was all he had ever really needed. The intimacies they shared at night were simply a side benefit.

The house had been sold, the minor packing already begun. Most of the removal detail would be taken care of by the firm Mark had hired, but her own things in particular she preferred to deal with herself. Leaving would be no wrench at all because she had never felt at home there. Perhaps because Diane had once lived there as Mark's wife; she wasn't sure. Whatever the reason, she couldn't wait for the day they said goodbye.

With her initial job done, Fiona no longer had reason to come to the house, but that hadn't stopped her. Tessa had become accustomed to hearing the silvery laugh and provocative tones on return from a shopping trip or a visit to the hairdressers. Not that she suspected Mark of organising any extra-marital activity on the premises. That far, he surely wouldn't stoop. She couldn't even be certain he was continuing the affair at all. One thing she refused to do was ask him. Chiefly, she admitted, for fear he would tell her what she didn't want to hear.

She spent the whole of that following Monday morning looking at carpets. Nothing fitted, not for this house. The waxed wood surrounds might mean more work, but the character of the place had to be preserved. She wouldn't be doing it herself, in any case, not if Mark had his way. Wives in his tax bracket didn't roughen their hands polishing and cleaning.

By lunch time, she was hungry enough to seek the in-store restaurant and eat what was for her a substantial meal of braised lamb. Refusing a sweet, she settled for coffee, taking out her list to check off the items already dealt with. She could, she knew, have employed an interior designer to take over all but the final decisions, but it was more fun this way. She would be putting her own stamp on the house.

For some time she had been aware on the very periphery of her vision of the woman seated at the next table, chiefly because the other seemed to be studying her. When she suddenly got up and came over, Tessa was half expecting a plea for some fund or other. Her actual words came as a total shock.

'I'm Mark's first wife, Diane. I couldn't pass up the chance to say hello.'

Looking up at the elegant figure in the off-white Chanel suit, Tessa felt her heart give a sickening little jerk. It was obvious, of course, that she would be a blue-eyed blonde, hence Jason's colouring, but her stunning good looks had somehow not been anticipated—or at least, not to this extent.

'How did you know me?' was all she could find to say in that first blank moment.

'I was at the wedding. Oh, not invited, of course,' with a faint smile. 'I just had to see the woman he finally replaced me with.' She drew out a chair without bothering to ask if Tessa minded. 'I hear he sold the house? Not before time. It must have fetched a pretty penny or two?'

Tessa felt her nostrils flare in instinctive dislike. 'I wouldn't know,' she said.

Perfectly shaped eyebrows lifted. 'That sounds like Mark. Keep it all close to the chest! I hope you weren't expecting a share and share alike type marriage. Parting Mark Leyland from his money is like squeezing blood from a stone!'

'Really?' Tessa was hard put to it to keep her tone from revealing her true reactions. 'I've always found him the most generous of men.' She added carefully, 'If you were at the church, you must have seen your son?'

'Jason? Yes, I saw him. Quite the little man, isn't he?' Her voice took on a harsher note. 'He could have saved my marriage!'

'At what cost to himself?' Tessa asked.

'I'm his mother.' Whatever softness there had been about the red mouth, it was gone now. 'I had the right!'

'But you left him. You left them both!'

'Blake didn't want children then. It's only this last year he started thinking about who he's going to leave it all to. I can't have any more.' She paused, biting her lower lip. 'Jason was my one chance to give him what he wanted.'

Tessa said softly, 'What makes you so sure he'd have accepted another man's child as his heir?'

'He'd agreed—until Mark came along and talked him out of going ahead with the suit.'

Brown eyes widened. 'Mark did? When?'

'Just a few days before the wedding. He was marrying a qualified children's nanny, he said. No court would listen to an unstable environment appeal with that factor in mind. Blake believed it. Now he's divorcing me to find himself a wife who can give him a son of his own!'

Tessa steeled herself against even the faintest spark of sympathy. 'I don't imagine you'll be left destitute.'

'I'll be taking him for every penny I can get!' The exclamation was vicious. 'I just wanted you to know what you've taken on. Mark Leyland lets nothing stand in the way of what *he* wants. He never did. He'll use anyone or anything!'

'He was fighting for Jason,' Tessa rejoined, closing her mind to the rest. 'And I think it best if you left now, because I really don't want to hear any more.'

'You'll learn.' Diane was in command of herself again, tone belittling. 'There'll be other women—if there aren't already—weeks when you won't even see him because he'll be off gathering material for those damned books of his! And you'll be left holding the baby—although at least he'll be in school most of the time and not tying you down!'

Tessa picked up the bill the waitress had left on the table when she had brought the coffee, and pressed herself to her feet.

'I have a lot to do,' she said with what calmness she could manage. 'I won't say it was nice meeting you, Diane, because it wouldn't be true.'

'I give you a year at the most,' came the contemptuous reply. 'Unless you get yourself pregnant pretty quick. A regular Sir Galahad is my ex when it comes to that sort of thing!'

She was still sitting there when Tessa had paid the bill at the desk and was leaving the restaurant, a warped and bitter woman whose looks had brought her little happiness. Everything she had said had been prompted by that bitterness, Tessa told herself; yet everything she had said had held at least a grain of truth. Mark would never in a million years have asked her to marry him if it hadn't been for Jason. But she already knew that, so why let it hurt?

She found it difficult to dissemble that evening when Jason was in bed and she and Mark were alone together. After receiving monosyllabic replies to his enquiries as to how the day had gone, he gave up, switching on the television to watch a current affairs programme.

Stretched out in the chair, feet comfortably crossed and hands clasped behind his head, he looked so relaxed, so totally unaffected by what was lacking in their marriage. To have him here at all was probably a bonus, Tessa reflected with cynicism. Once they moved out to Rylands he would no doubt start finding excuses to stop over in town for the odd night.

At least the book was finished. That in itself had been a surprise. Researching another would probably mean weeks of travel to come though. And why not? she asked herself. He had no worries now about leaving Jason, and he certainly wouldn't be too concerned about leaving her!

'I thought I might go over to see Laura and Roger this weekend,' she said when the credits came on. 'Roger's off to the States again next week, so there may not be another opportunity to get them together for some time.'

'Good idea,' he returned. 'Take the car. I can always use taxis if I need to.'

Obviously he had no intention of coming with her. 'You'd like me to take Jason with me, then?' she asked. 'I thought you might prefer a little time alone together.'

'There are one or two things I have to do this weekend.' His tone was evasive.

'Which could as easily be done during the week, I'm sure.' It was for Jason she was angry now. 'You spend hardly any time at all with him, Mark! Surely you can spare one day?'

He had come upright in the chair, his whole manner altered. 'Are you trying to tell me how I should treat my own son?'

She flared immediately, too incensed to consider her words. 'Marrying a permanent housekeeper doesn't let you off the hook. Diane was right about you. You're only interested in your own needs!'

The lean features were suddenly mask-like. 'Diane?'

Tessa held his gaze. Too late now to retract; why bother, anyway? 'We met in Harrods this lunch time.'

'By arrangement?'

'By chance. She was at the wedding, did you know that? She recognised me from then.'

'And, being Diane, couldn't resist the opportunity to put in the knife.' His voice had gained a rougher edge. 'What exactly did she have to say?'

'Nothing I didn't already know—apart from the fact that you'd been to see her husband and talk him out of continuing the suit. He's divorcing her now so that he can have a son by someone else.'

'And I'm supposed to feel guilty about that?'

She shook her head. 'Of course not. She hardly deserves any better.' Tone hardening a fraction, she added, 'On the other hand, something had to make her the way she is.'

'Try nature.' Mark was angry but in control of it, his mouth a thin, tight line. 'Diane is incapable of feeling anything for anyone. Something lacking in her make-up. Heaven knows, I've little enough to be proud of myself in regard to the relationship we had, but she was the one to walk away from it.'

'Perhaps if you hadn't been so busy travelling the world, she might have stayed with it,' Tessa retorted. 'Few women like being left to bring up a baby on their own.'

'Few women could walk out and leave a three-year-old child on *its* own,' he came back brusquely. 'If I hadn't been turned back by bad weather at the airport that day there might have been a real tragedy.'

Tessa felt the fire die out of her. 'I—didn't realise.'

'There's a lot you don't realise.' He was speaking in clipped, precise tones. 'So maybe it's time I told you.'

'You don't have to,' she protested. 'You really don't, Mark!'

He looked at her for a long moment, face losing little of its hardness. 'Yes, I do. It wasn't very much more than a casual affair initially. We met at some party or other. I was on the point of calling it a day when she told me she was pregnant. We were married within the week. Register office, of course.' The smile lacked humour. 'One of the reasons I didn't put up too much objection to the fuss and palaver this time. We'd little or nothing in common. Not even much of a physical interest by then. It got worse after Jason was born. I think he was around six months old when she told me it was quite possible that he wasn't even my son.'

'Oh, no!' Tessa hardly knew what else to say. 'She was lying, of course!'

'Perhaps. Then again, perhaps not. He certainly doesn't resemble me.'

No, she thought, he resembled his mother—in looks, if nothing else.

'And that's why you found it difficult to be around either of them too much?' she murmured. 'I can appreciate that now. What convinced you in the end?'

'Convinced me?'

'That Jason really is your son?'

The shrug was brief. 'I don't suppose I ever will be wholly sure. It doesn't seem to matter that much any more. He's mine in name, and I love him. I simply didn't realise just how much until there was a risk of losing him. I've been far from the perfect father all round.'

'So who's perfect?' she asked softly. 'I shouldn't have tried to pressure you.'

There was a pause, a slight lessening of obduracy. 'No, you were right about that, too. I haven't spent enough time with him. It will be different when we move to Rylands.'

'Until you go material-gathering for the next book.' She couldn't hold back on that comment. 'Thailand, didn't you say?'

'Some time, maybe. I thought I might try something different.'

Her heart gave a leap. 'Such as?'

'It's said everyone has at least one novel in them. I've had the makings turning over in my mind for the past year. The setting will be England, so I shan't need to go far afield for my background material.' He slanted a lip at the expression on her face. 'Is the relief just for Jason's sake, or do I take it you'll be glad to have me around more too?'

'Of course I shall!' She wanted badly to go to him, to show her feelings in action if not in actual words, but something inside her still held back. At least she could understand him a little better now. Understand, and sympathise. Diane was amoral; she simply had no standards by which she could be judged. As much to be pitied as despised. 'We'll be making a new start,' she added with purpose, closing her mind to Fiona's intruding image. Trust had to start somewhere. Let it be here.

'Then let's hope we make a better job of it than the first,' he responded. 'Talking of new starts, my publishers are holding their annual soirée Thursday evening. I already said we'd be there.'

At least Fiona would have no reason to be, Tessa reflected swiftly. 'What about Jason?' she asked.

'We'll bring in a reliable sitter for the evening—and other evenings too, if it comes to that. You can't spend the next few years sitting around waiting for him to grow up enough to leave on his own.'

'I don't mind.'

'But I do.' His tone was suddenly brusque again. 'If we're going to make this marriage of ours work at all, then there has to be effort from both sides. Jason won't come to any harm for being left occasionally.'

He had a valid point, Tessa knew. Valid *and* encouraging. She would make any effort towards achieving a better relationship.

'All right,' she said, 'I'll contact the agency in the morning. They keep a file of vetted sitters.'

'Do that.' He moved his gaze from her face slowly down over her slender shape, the expression in his eyes setting her heart hammering in a manner only too familiar. 'I feel like an early night,' he announced. 'How about you?'

She could hardly hear her voice through the blood pounding like surf in her ears. 'That sounds like a good idea.'

In this way he never failed her, she thought mistily a long time later when she lay limp and enervated in his arms. If only she weren't so much aware that for a man the act itself was satisfaction enough. If it took a lifetime she would make him love her, she vowed before finally drifting off to sleep to the sound and feel of his steady breathing.

CHAPTER TEN

THE soirée, as Mark termed it, was held at the publishing house itself. Wearing the classic little black dress that had cost her more than a week's salary just a few short months ago, Tessa found herself able to cope with any conversational overtures that came her way, despite all her misgivings. The directors themselves went out of their way to make her and the other guests feel at home amid the motley collection of novelists and non-fiction writers which constituted their 'stable'.

Mark himself was highly thought of both as man and author, she gathered from the public relations officer who was young and go ahead and brimming over with enthusiasm for his job. His cup would runneth over, he declared extravagantly, if she could persuade her husband to consent to the occasional signing session on publication of a new book. Women in particular were swayed by the personal dedication, especially when it came from an author with Mark's brand of charisma. All it took was a few words, a smile, and he would have that reader for life.

'If the book's worth reading, they'll buy it anyway,' said Mark drily in the taxi taking them on to dinner when Tessa mentioned the conversation. 'Signing sessions are the pits!'

'Amen to that!' agreed the man seated on one of the pull-down seats opposite with feeling. 'Stewart talked me into doing one on my last book. I sat there for four hours and only two old dears turned up!'

'Death to the artistic ego,' observed his partner, winking at Tessa with a hint of conspiracy. 'Who'd be married to a writer?'

I would, she thought, feeling the warmth and firmness of Mark's arm against hers as the vehicle rounded a corner. But then, it wouldn't matter what he was; he would still arouse the same emotions.

'Shall you be offering the novel to the same publishers?' she asked later when they were dancing to the strains of the resident band.

'Doubtful,' he acknowledged. 'It isn't going to be in their line.'

'I'll look forward to reading it,' she said, and saw his mouth widen briefly as he glanced down at her.

'That's looking a long way ahead. I might not be any good at novel writing. It's a totally different technique.'

'There's nothing to be lost by trying.'

'No.' There was an odd note in his voice. 'Perseverance is the keynote.'

Tessa hoped he was right in that, and not just where writing was concerned, either. With his arms about her she felt content for the moment. He looked so devastatingly attractive in the dark grey suit. Other women thought so, too; it was there in the sidelong glances, the sly little smiles. Only she was the one who wore his ring. No matter what happened, she would never take it off.

Out of all the people who had been at the gathering earlier, only four, plus their respective partners, had been invited along here. Tessa was talking to one of the other wives when she saw Fiona enter the restaurant with Dean close at her back.

The former was wearing a designer creation in black and white that had heads turning in the vicinity. Mark had seen them too, Tessa noted, glancing sideways along the table; his eyes were narrowed, his whole bearing stiffened. That he hadn't expected to see the two of them was obvious—that he didn't like what he saw equally so.

The *maître d'* approached the newcomers, regretfully shaking his head in reply to Dean's apparent request for a table, the sweep of his hand an invitation to observe the full complement of diners.

'Isn't that your brother, Mark?' asked Philip Jamieson, the editorial director. 'Ask them over. We can fit in another couple of chairs.'

Short of refusing point-blank, Tessa supposed he had little choice but act on the invitation. Numbly she watched him move across the room to intercede, saw Fiona turn to greet him and knew that for her the whole evening had gone sour. Then the three of them were coming over, Fiona thanking Philip with a smile that sent his blood-pressure soaring, to judge from the flush elicited.

'Quite a long time since we last met,' he said jovially to Dean as the two took the seats quickly procured. 'Canada not to your liking, then?'

'You could say that,' agreed the younger man, revealing no sign of discomfiture. 'This is decent of you. I didn't expect reservations to be necessary at this time of the week.'

'You've been away too long,' declared Fiona on a lightly jesting note. Her eyes sought Mark's across the table, expression difficult to assess. 'Have you decided on a removal date yet?'

'Three weeks today,' he acknowledged. 'The decorators will have finished by then.'

'So we can look forward to a housewarming in the not too distant future,' put in Philip with the ease of long acquaintance. 'Plus a new opus, hopefully. You wrote this last one in record time, Mark!'

'I had pretty comprehensive notes to work from,' came the reply.

'Plus the incentive of a wedding coming up,' commented Dean on a bland note. 'Who wants to think of mundane things like work on honeymoon?'

'But as I shan't be getting married every six months, don't expect the same schedule on any others,' advised his brother with irony amid general laughter. 'I might even take a sabbatical.'

'Not too long a one, I hope,' Philip rejoined. 'The non-fiction list would suffer greatly without a regular Leyland to boost it.'

Tessa sat there and let the conversation wash over her, a smile fixed to her lips. She felt tired and listless, aware of the dull ache under her ribs. None of this was coincidence; Fiona had known where Mark was going to be tonight, and only he could have told her. If she was using Dean just to arouse Mark's jealousy, then surely Dean himself must realise it?

Unless he was simply lending himself to the situation in order to get back at his brother for throwing him out. That would be like him—or at least what she knew of him.

She kept the smile going when Mark asked Fiona to dance, but was hard put to it to do so when Dean suggested they do the same. Had it not been for revealing her feelings about her brother-in-law to the others at the table, she would have turned him down flat. As it was, she could only put on an act of normality and allow him to lead her on to the floor.

'I owe you an apology,' he said softly after a moment or two of frigid silence on her part. 'That was a lousy trick I played on you. Put it down to jealousy, pure and simple.'

Tessa looked him straight in the eye, but there was no hint of mockery in his expression. 'Jealousy?'

'Because Mark found you first. Girls like you are few and far between, Tessa. It took me a while to realise you weren't like all the others—out for what you could get.'

She said emphatically, 'I'm not sure what the game is, Dean, but it won't wash. You wanted to ruin things for us.'

'Of course I did. Mark always had all the good breaks. I don't think he deserves you.'

Flattery perhaps, but it struck a chord. Over his shoulder she caught a glimpse of a dark head bent close to a blonde one. When she spoke again, it was without the anger. 'How come you're with Fiona?'

'I'm staying at her place,' he said. 'I'd nowhere else to go after Mark tossed me out on my ear.'

'Does he know?'

'He probably does now. Sheer bad luck I had to choose this place.'

Her head jerked. '*You* chose it?'

'That's right.' His laugh held a wry note. 'Although Fiona's doing the paying, I have to admit.'

'You'll neither of you have to now,' she said with purpose. 'You're invited guests.'

'At these prices, that has to be a bonus.' There was a pause, a change of tone. 'Tessa, I know I don't merit it, but will you do something for me?'

She was cautious. 'What?'

'I need money. Enough to tide me over until I find a job. I can't keep sponging off Fiona.'

'You want me to lend you money?'

'Not you—Mark.'

'You could ask him yourself,' she said pointedly. 'He's your brother.'

'And a hard nut to crack, as you probably know.'

'So why assume he'll listen to anything I can say—especially after the impression you left him with the other night?'

'He's no fool. He'd have had my guts for garters if he'd really believed there was anything in it.' His voice took on a certain desperation. 'I'm at rock bottom, Tessa. Living off a woman is no easy thing for a man.'

'I'm sure.' She tried hard to keep any trace of satire from her voice. What he was asking was too much. There was no way she was going to jeopardise her own position by suggesting to Mark that her interest in his brother was strong enough to elicit such support. Yet at the same time she had to feel some sympathy with Dean's predicament. She added slowly, 'How much would you need?'

'A couple of thousand would give me a breathing space.' He sounded suddenly hopeful. 'You're a gem, Tessa!'

She was a fool, she thought wryly. Two thousand would almost clean out her readily available assets. All the same, if it hadn't been for her, he and Mark might never have become estranged. She hardly needed it, anyway. She had a husband to take care of her now.

'How would you want the money?' she asked.

'A cheque paid into my bank would be fine. I opened the account with my last few pounds in the hope that I could talk them into a loan, but they weren't playing. If they saw that kind of money going in it would up my credibility no end.'

'I'll see what I can do,' she promised. 'You'd better let me have the name and branch address just in case.'

'It's Lloyds on Old Bond Street.'

The music came to an end. Dean stood for a brief moment looking down at her, an odd expression in his eyes. 'Mark's a lucky man,' he said, and pressed his lips swiftly to her temple. 'I hope he realises it.'

The other two were back at the table before them. Mark watched them coming, expression unreadable. There was a self-satisfied look about Fiona's red mouth.

The latter danced the next number or two with Philip, whose bemusement seemed to grow by the minute as he gazed into the upturned, provocatively smiling face. Glenda Jamieson appeared to be taking little note, but, sensitised herself to such emotions, Tessa could guess how she was really feeling.

There was no telling what Mark was thinking; the spark in his eyes could be anger, disgust or even amusement. When the party eventually began to break up around twelve-thirty, he seemed in no particular hurry to join the exodus. Only when Glenda herself confessed to a certain readiness to call it a day did he take steps to ensure a swift conclusion by suggesting that Fiona and Dean share a taxi with them.

For Tessa at least, it was an uncomfortable ride. Fiona herself seemed unaware of any atmosphere, keeping up a light conversation the whole way out to Hampstead where she had her flat, and which Mark had insisted on going to first. He made no comment when Dean alighted there too, although Tessa saw his lips compress.

'I'll be in touch,' he said.

He spoke little until they reached the house. The sitter sent by the agency was staying the night, but came down on hearing them to say that Jason had fallen on the stairs and banged his head.

'He was sick after it, so I sent for the emergency doctor,' she said. 'He doesn't think there's any real damage done, but wants a close eye kept on him over the next thirty-six hours or so.' She added apologetically, 'I really am sorry. I can't think how it happened.'

'Just one of those things,' Tessa assured her, controlling the urge to rush straight upstairs and check for herself on Jason's condition. 'You were right to call the doctor.'

'I'll give Lawrence Gordon a ring first thing in the morning and let him have a look at him,' said Mark after the girl had gone back to her room. 'He's treated him since he was a baby.'

'Harley Street, I suppose?' queried Tessa on a gibing note.

'Close enough,' he returned levelly. 'Don't knock what you don't know. He's an excellent physician.'

She ignored the injunction, turning away towards the stairs. 'I'm going to have a look at him. Are you coming?'

'If he's asleep, two of us are more likely to waken him,' he said. 'I'll trust your judgement.'

Which made sense, except that Tessa wasn't prepared to see it that way. 'Typical of your attitude,' she snapped, and left him standing there.

Jason was asleep. He looked peaceful enough, she conceded, his forehead cool and dry. The bruise was just above his right temple, the skin already threatening extensive discoloration. A second opinion was obviously a good idea. One couldn't be too careful with head injuries of any kind.

She dropped a kiss on the sleeping face before leaving him. The way things were shaping, he was the one reliable quality in the whole family. If nothing else kept her from giving up on this marriage of hers, Jason would.

Mark was in the bathroom; she could hear water running. She undressed swiftly and pulled on a wrap before putting away the black dress and shoes in the wardrobe. The grey suit lay where he had dropped it on the bed. Tessa put that away, too. Quite the little housewife, she thought derisively. Would Fiona bother to tidy up after a man?

He was wearing the silk robe when he eventually emerged. 'Everything OK?' he asked.

'On the face of it.' Despite all efforts, she couldn't quite eradicate the brittleness. 'I'll feel better after Dr Gordon sees him.'

One eyebrow lifted sardonically, but he made no comment. He peeled off the robe with his back to her, arousing the usual emotions at the sight of that lean, hard body. Snatching up the clean nightdress she had got out ready, Tessa went into the bathroom and closed the door between them. The barriers were up and they were staying up. Let him go to Fiona for solace.

She had thought him asleep when she finally slid into bed. When he spoke she jumped, heart missing a beat.

'Are you trying to tell me something?'

'I'm not sure what you mean,' she murmured, and sensed the curl of his lip.

'Why the nightdress?'

'Because I'm tired,' she said, giving up on the former line. 'In more ways than the one,' she tagged on meaningfully.

His laugh was short. 'First wait till you're asked,' he said, and rolled on to his side away from her. 'Sweet dreams.'

Coward! she told herself bitterly as his breathing steadied. She should have spoken her mind regarding Fiona's presence at the restaurant tonight. He must have told her they were going to be there, yet with what purpose in mind? He hadn't been expecting her to turn up with Dean in tow, that was for sure.

'I suppose you do realise they're living together?' she said with malice into the darkness.

'Go to sleep.' His voice was expressionless. 'You need your rest.'

Dr Gordon arrived at ten-thirty and gave Jason a thorough examination, making a game of it so as not to alarm him too much.

'No problems that I can see,' he pronounced in the end, putting the ophthalmoscope back in his bag. 'Probably just a mild concussion.' He ruffled the thick fair hair. 'Try taking water with your whisky in future, eh, laddie!'

'I only had drinking chocolate,' returned Jason, taking the injunction seriously. 'I've never tasted whisky.'

The doctor hid a smile. 'I'd keep it that way, too,' he advised. 'There's nothing worse than waking up with a thick head!'

'Would you like some coffee?' asked Tessa hastily, seeing the question trembling on Jason's lips. 'It's all ready.'

'Sounds good,' he agreed. 'I don't have any more calls.'

He stayed for half an hour, a big, bluff Scot Tessa couldn't help but like. In his late fifties, he had been the family physician for the past twenty-five years, she learned, and his father another thirty before that. He was sorry to hear they were leaving town. It would, he said, be like losing a part of his own family.

'You'll still be the man we'll call on for anything but emergencies,' Mark told him easily. 'You don't give up fifty-odd years of trust for a few miles of travel. In any case, you must come out and visit us—you *and* Dorothy.'

He disappeared into the study as soon as the doctor left, emerging again at twelve to announce he would be eating out. He didn't say where, or with whom, and Tessa had no intention of asking. The atmosphere between them was frigid, but she wasn't going to be the one to break the ice.

Laura was delighted to see her, Roger equally so. Theirs was an excellent, well-balanced marriage—perhaps lacking a little inasmuch as Roger spent so much time away from home; but it was his job, after all, and not just by choice. It gave them all the material assets they could want, including a beautiful home.

'I'm looking forward to seeing Rylands,' Laura confessed when the sisters managed to snatch a few moments alone together while Roger played football with all three children in the garden. 'It sounds out of this world!' She studied Tessa's face, her expression a little uncertain. 'Is anything wrong?' she asked.

Tessa summoned a smile, mentally chiding herself for allowing her inner feelings to show. 'Everything's fine,' she lied. 'I'm just a bit tired, that's all.'

Laura looked relieved. 'Of course. Silly of me. Organising a new house is always a traumatic time, especially when it has to be done from a distance. When do you actually take possession of the keys?'

'Wednesday. The decorators move in on Thursday, the furnishings a fortnight after that.'

'Lucky you, to be starting off with everything done! I'll bet you can hardly wait to see it all finished?'

Pretending enthusiasm for something she felt so totally unimportant right now was difficult. Tessa did the best she could, but from the slight frown between Laura's brows it seemed she wasn't wholly convincing.

'I suppose it will all come together once we're there,' she said in the end. 'The boys sound as if they're having a good time!"

Laura accepted the change of subject without comment. 'Roger, too. He'd like us to have another.'

Tessa glanced at her swiftly. 'You're not too keen on the idea?'

She laughed. 'I might be if I could be guaranteed a girl next time! Not that I'd be without either of my boys,' she added fondly. 'Just that it would be nice to buy dresses and ribbons for a change. What about you? Would you want a boy or a girl yourself?'

'I hadn't really thought about it,' answered Tessa, this time managing to keep her tone suitably buoyant. 'I've promised Jason he can have a puppy when we move to the new house. That seems enough to be going on with.'

'I'd say so!' Laura pulled a face. 'Dirty feet, and puddles all over the floor—and that's if you're lucky!'

'Yes, well, they soon grow out of that stage.'

'And into even bigger liabilities. Anyway, let's get lunch on the table. I've a feeling they're all going to be trooping in any minute yelling for sustenance.'

Tessa had intimated to Mark that they would be staying the whole day, and for supper, but by four-thirty she could take the strain of pretending all was well with her world no longer. Jason said a lofty goodbye to his young stepcousins. When he was in his new house, he declared, they must come and visit with him. He might even let them play with his puppy!

'I've a feeling I'm going to be fighting a losing battle against having one of our own,' exclaimed Laura in wry aside as she kissed Tessa. 'Trust you to set the pattern!'

Tessa laughed. 'I didn't, Kim did. Anyway, it will give you something to do when Roger's away.' She closed the window, waving a hand. 'See you soon!'

They hit a considerable amount of traffic on the way in, and the afternoon had given way to evening before they eventually turned the corner into Ranleigh Gardens.

The black Porsche parked in their allotted space was too familiar for there to be any doubt about ownership.

Without pausing for consideration, she pressed down jerkily on the accelerator, moving on past the house and round the far corner. So she had proof at last, she thought numbly. They were in there right now, the two of them; perhaps even in the bed she had shared with him.

'Tessa?' Jason was both surprised and perturbed by the sudden change of plan. 'Did you forget something?'

From somewhere she found the ability to smile and shake her head. 'I just don't feel like going indoors just yet. How about going up to see Peter Pan?'

He was puzzled still, but amenable. 'All right.'

Kensington Gardens were lovely in their autumn colours. After viewing the statue, they walked over and spent twenty minutes or so watching the children sailing model boats on the Round Pond. It was Jason's growing restlessness that settled the issue in the end. If Fiona was still there when they got back, then the confrontation would be immediate, that was all. If the car had gone, it would depend on what Mark had to say. She was, Tessa told herself, prepared to give him the benefit of the doubt that far, providing he mentioned the visit at all.

Her pent-up breath came out on a sigh when they turned the corner again to find the space empty. Parking with care, she locked all doors before making slowly for the house. Jason was first inside.

'Daddy, we're home!' he called.

Mark appeared in the study doorway. He seemed perfectly at ease. 'Had a good day?' he asked.

'Fine,' Tessa replied, and wondered at her own natural sound. 'And you?'

'Quiet,' he acknowledged. 'I thought you said you'd be staying for supper?'

Jason had disappeared into the drawing-room. Mentally excusing herself for the white lie, she said, 'Jason wanted to get back in time for that quiz programme. You know how he loves answering the questions.'

'Especially when he beats the contestants.' His regard was steady, his thoughts his own. 'Are you feeling all right?'

'Fine,' she said again, not bothering to keep the acidity under wraps. 'I'll see about something to eat.'

It being Saturday, Jason had an extra hour before being despatched to bed. Coming downstairs again after looking in on him, Tessa went straight through to the kitchen to make coffee. All through the evening, she had waited for Mark to mention Fiona's visit, but she had waited in vain. If that didn't point to his guilt, nothing did. What she was going to do about it, she wasn't yet sure. Walking out on him was no solution. Not with Jason to consider. She had to face him with it, let him see she wasn't prepared to be made a fool of any more.

'I think it's about time we sorted ourselves out,' he said brusquely from the doorway behind her, startling her because she hadn't heard him come in. 'I don't know what game we're supposed to be playing, but . . .'

'You're the one doing the playing,' she interrupted without turning. She let the pause stand for a pointed moment. 'I saw Fiona's car outside earlier.'

The silence seemed to stretch for an age. When he did speak, it was on a flat note. 'You just underlined the very reason I didn't tell you she'd been here.'

'Circumstantial evidence again?' This time she did swing round, eyes blazing. 'Don't give me that, Mark! You thought I was out of the way for another couple of hours!'

'In which case, isn't it surprising she left as soon as she did?' He made a sudden impatient gesture. 'I'm not going to waste my time trying to convince you. You've obviously already made up your mind.'

'So what am I supposed to do, just forget it?'

The shrug was deliberate in its suggestion of indifference. 'Do as you think fit.'

'You've got me over a barrel, haven't you?' she said bitterly. 'You know I'm not going to walk out of here!'

'Because of Jason? Yes, I know. It's your one redeeming feature.'

The hurt went too deep for rational thought—or behaviour. All she wanted was to get back at him. 'In that case, perhaps you'd better start paying me again as his nanny, because that's all I'm going to be in this house from now on!'

Grey eyes blazed into sudden frightening life. He reached her before she could move, taking her by the shoulders and dragging her up to him. She had never been kissed with such savagery before, his teeth biting into her lower lip until she felt the salt taste of blood in her mouth. He was aroused; she could feel that too. Only this was no tender lover out to share an emotion, this was a man intent on dealing out retribution.

'You're my wife,' he gritted, pinning her up against the wall with the hard weight of his body. 'You're supposed to have trust!'

'I do,' she spat at him. 'I trust you to be what you are—a liar and a cheat! You want the best of both worlds, Mark. Well, you're not having it with me! You can repeat the performance you put on in Guernsey, of course, but so can I. And I will. As many times as it takes to convince you I'm not here just to be used when it suits you!'

He was looking at her as if he'd never seen her before, his face grimly set. 'If that's the way you feel, there's no point in making the effort,' he said, and let her go. 'Just do your job, and we'll both be happy.'

That was a state she was never going to achieve again, she thought numbly as he turned away. To all intents and purposes, the marriage was over.

CHAPTER ELEVEN

WITHIN a week of moving to Rylands, Tessa felt as though she had lived there all her life. Jason too was in his element. Getting him in from the wonderland of a garden for meals proved quite a task.

Aware of how frustrating the word 'soon' was to a child, Tessa made arrangements to fetch the Retriever puppy from the breeders the second weekend. Having shown little initial interest in the proposal, even Mark himself was captivated by the golden bundle of mischief Jason christened Corey.

Boy and dog became instantly inseparable. It was only with the greatest difficulty that Tessa could persuade the former to leave the latter downstairs at bed time. Once housetrained, she promised, the animal would be allowed a basket in the bedroom.

'Kim's predecessor always slept in my room,' she defended when Mark queried the hygiene of such an arrangement, 'and I never picked anything up.'

'You obviously over-indulge animals the same way you do children,' came the dry response. 'Let's hope Mrs Horsley holds the same views. Finding someone else might prove difficult.'

Tessa had flatly refused to look for a housekeeper, settling instead for the daily help used for many years by Mrs Pierce. In her mid-sixties, the woman was a grandmother several times over, and seemed to take most things in her stride. It was doubtful, Tessa thought, that she would regard a few dog hairs as any great drawback.

'I'll handle it,' she returned coolly. 'And before you disappear into the study for the rest of the evening, hadn't we better talk about the housewarming party?'

About to get up from his chair, Mark paused to look at her enquiringly. 'What housewarming party?'

Tessa kept her expression strictly neutral. 'The one you promised to invite Philip Jamieson to.'

'You mean the one he assumed we'd be giving.'

'Whichever, it was a nice idea.' She added with emphasis, 'Unless you have definite objections, of course?'

His shrug suggested indifference, his tone confirmed it. 'It's entirely up to you.'

'I have to know who you'll want inviting,' she insisted, and hesitated just a moment before tagging on, 'What about Dean, for instance?'

There was no discernible change of expression in the grey eyes. 'Why not?'

'And—Fiona?'

The thinning of his lips told its own story. 'Just let me know the date you settle on and I'll see to my end of it.'

Tessa sat disconsolately viewing the rest of the lonely evening as he went from the room. He had started work on the novel almost immediately after they'd moved in, and spent most of his time shut in the study. Since the night she had accused him of continuing his affair with Fiona, there had been no intimacy between them of any kind. They occupied the same house, even the same bed, but were as far apart as any two people could be.

In many ways, it would have been so much better for both of them had this marriage really been one of convenience only, she thought bleakly. Unconsummated, her feelings for him would have died a natural death in time.

Better, in any case, to suffer lack of fulfilment than this gnawing loss.

Whether he was still in touch with Fiona or not, she had no way of knowing. He had been up to town a couple of times since their move out here, although he hadn't stayed overnight. If only for Jason's sake, she couldn't contemplate leaving him, yet the thought of spending the next five or six years in this kind of limbo was more than she could bear either. There had to come a point at which they came to some kind of understanding, though how that was to be arrived at she had no idea.

She was in bed and feigning sleep as usual when Mark eventually came up. The super-sized bed was wide enough for them both to stay in their respective halves without touching at any point. With the lights out, silence reigned for all of five minutes before Corey started crying for his mother's warmth and comfort: a plaintive sound that stirred Tessa into immediate response.

'Leave him,' Mark said quietly as she made to slide from the bed. 'He has to learn to be on his own some time.'

'He's only eight weeks old!' she protested.

'And likely to keep up the same racket as long as it gets results.' He rolled to reach for her arm when she continued to get up, pulling her back down again with a force that shook her. 'I said leave him!'

'Don't take your frustration out on a helpless animal!' she shot at him. 'And take your hands off me!'

'You think I'm suffering from frustration?' he asked hardily, ignoring the latter injunction. 'Well, that's a matter easily rectified!'

Flat on her back, she felt his weight come over her— felt the heat of his body burning into her. His mouth was merciless, forcing open her lips and bruising the tender flesh inside, his hands like vices, pinning her arms to the pillows as she tried to push him away.

She was wearing a nightdress, but it was no protection against this kind of intent. She fought him savagely, desisting only when she realised that her struggles were simply goading him into further efforts.

'Is rape all you can come up with?' she hissed. 'I don't want you, Mark! Can't you get that through your head?'

'Like hell you don't.' His eyes glittered in the moonlit darkness. 'Do you think I can't recognise arousal in a woman when I feel it?'

'You should do.' She was past caring what she flung at him now. 'I'm sure you've had enough practice!'

He stopped her mouth at that point by the simple expedient of covering it with his own. Tessa felt the thin material of her nightdress tear as he pulled at it, and suddenly stopped caring about keeping him at arm's length. It had been so long since they'd been together. She couldn't go on fighting him. Not like this.

He made a small sound of satisfaction deep in his throat as he felt her soften in his arms and begin to respond. His body was hard, demanding, allowing her no quarter as he pressured open her thighs. Passion flooded out all other considerations as she took him into her, the moan wrung from her lips a plea not a protest, the bruising strength of him filling the emptiness of these past lonely weeks as if they had never been.

She was grateful when he made no immediate attempt to move away from her after it was over. If they didn't seize this opportunity to try straightening things out, there might never be another, she thought. Regardless of what he had or hadn't done, she loved this man whose dark head lay against her breast.

'We have to talk,' he murmured at length, echoing her thoughts.

'I know.' Tessa steeled herself to go on. 'I realise I'm no match for someone like Fiona, Mark, but neither am I willing to play the role so many other wives play. If you'll promise not to see her any more, I'll take your word on it.'

It was a moment or two before he replied. When he did, it was on a note that made her heart sink again. 'I doubt it. If you had any trust in me at all, you wouldn't need to ask for any promises.'

'All I want,' she said desperately as he shifted his weight from her, 'is some kind of assurance. Fiona is very beautiful, I know, but——'

'She's very beautiful—period.' His tone was sardonic. 'Few men could look at her and not feel stirred. You don't need a man, Tessa, you need a saint!'

'That's not true.' Her throat hurt. 'Feeling is one thing, acting on it another. I managed to come to terms with what happened during that fortnight before the wedding——'

'Such magnanimity,' he mocked. 'Let's take the rest as read, shall we?'

'We can't just leave it there,' she protested.

'Yes, we can.' He was already settling down again, his back to her. 'You either trust me or you don't. I'm not wasting any more breath on the subject.'

Corey had stopped crying, she realised, gazing numbly at the shadowed ceiling. If he could accept his lot, perhaps she should too. Mark hadn't said he wouldn't be seeing Fiona again, but neither had he said he would. She had to give the latter option credibility unless or until proved otherwise.

*   *   *

Preparations for the party took up most of her waking hours during the days following. It was for that reason alone that she had decided against hiring a firm of caterers, preferring to turn her own mind and hand to the buffet supper she had thought most appropriate to the occasion.

Mark made no particular comment other than to suggest she kept it reasonably simple. Work on the novel appeared to have been shelved for the present; whether from choice or lack of inspiration, Tessa wasn't sure and hesitated to ask. Their whole relationship was balanced on a knife-edge. The last thing she wanted was to risk tipping it the wrong way.

Only at night, when he made love to her, was she able to feel any real sense of security. At the very least she could rouse that much emotion in him. She would make him forget Fiona, she vowed with slowly growing confidence when he showed no inclination to go up to town. All she needed was time.

Replies to the invitations she had sent out were swiftly forthcoming. Out of the thirty-six people asked, only one couple said regretfully that they couldn't make it. There was no word from Fiona, but then she would obviously reply directly to Mark, Tessa told herself. She would be here, nothing was surer.

Laura and Roger were to pick up Tessa's parents. At Mark's suggestion, the four of them were to stay the night. With three bedrooms standing empty, he said, there was no reason why relatives shouldn't benefit.

'That still leaves one free,' Tessa pointed out a little diffidently on the Friday evening. 'How about Dean? He's a relative, too.'

'Depends whether he brings anyone with him.' Grey eyes met brown with faint cynicism. 'Or wouldn't it bother you to have him share with some girlfriend?'

Tessa made herself hold his gaze. 'I hadn't thought about it,' she acknowledged. 'He didn't say he was bringing anyone when he phoned.'

Mark's regard sharpened. 'When did he phone?'

'While you were taking Corey round the garden this afternoon. I meant to mention it, but I forgot.'

'Too much else on your mind, I suppose.' The pause was brief. 'So, what else did he have to say?'

'Not a lot.' She heard the evasive quality in her voice and made an effort to eradicate it. 'You knew he'd taken a flat, of course?'

'No, I didn't. So he finally found himself a job?'

'He's been short-listed for one—financial consultant with an investment company.'

'Sounds right up his street—always providing his clients are prepared to withstand more losses than gains.' He added thoughtfully, 'It would be interesting to know how he got hold of the funds to lease a flat. I've been anticipating an appeal for weeks.'

Tessa herself had wondered how Dean had managed to make two thousand pounds stretch over more than a month of the kind of living standards he considered essential to his well being. She had paid the cheque into his account and the sum had been duly deducted from her own, that was all she knew. The matter hadn't been mentioned this afternoon, which was typical, she supposed, of Dean's attitude to life. Why should he feel gratitude for a handout from a brother who had so much more than he had?

'Would you have responded to it if he'd made one?' she asked on what she hoped was a casual note.

'Possibly. It would have depended on his future plans.'

Meaning if he'd still been with Fiona the answer would have been no, she surmised. Which fact in itself suggested a retention of interest.

'Let's play it by ear,' she said, controlling the reaction elicited by that thought. 'If he comes alone, he stays.'

His shrug dismissed the subject. 'Whatever you like.'

For the party, Tessa had bought a simple sheath of a dress in natural wild silk which skimmed rather than clung to her figure. With her hair taken up from her face and piled into glossy abundance on top of her head, she looked taller and somehow more mature when she viewed herself in the bedroom mirror on Saturday evening. Not a patch on the way Fiona would no doubt look, of course, she reflected, then resolutely put the woman out of her mind.

Mark was adding the final touches to the fruit punch for those who would be driving. Some unreadable expression flickered across his face as he looked up and saw her standing in the doorway.

'Good timing,' he said. 'That sounds like a car.'

Her own family were the first arrivals. Both Laura and her mother were openly and genuinely taken with the house. Tessa had felt guilty over not inviting them over before this, but circumstances had been such that she hadn't wanted anyone around who knew her well enough to guess that all was not perfect with her new world.

People came in droves over the next half-hour. Those who couldn't get on the drive parked along the lane, which was fortunately unrestricted. By nine-o'clock the whole house was humming with sound as groups were formed and conversations got under way.

Dean was one of the last to arrive. He had on a suit that was obviously new, and just as obviously expensive.

'I got the job!' he exclaimed, presenting Tessa with the magnificent bouquet of roses he was carrying. 'That's just to say thanks. You too, of course,' he added to his brother who was standing by. 'I never really expected you to come through.'

'I'll put these straight into water,' Tessa said hastily, seeing Mark's face change. Explanations could wait until they were alone.

Fiona was probably delaying her appearance in order to make an entrance, she thought, filling a vase at the kitchen tap. Meeting the other woman again would have been so much easier had she only been sure Mark wasn't seeing her privately. Trust me, he'd said, but how could she? Leopards didn't change their spots overnight.

By ten-thirty, with still no sign of the missing guest, Tessa could only assume she wouldn't after all be coming. It was the why that puzzled her most. Surely Mark would have made some mention of a refusal?

In the meantime, however, she had other matters to occupy her mind. The party was going with a swing. Some people were already dancing to taped music in the smaller sitting-room, others beginning to filter through to the dining-room where the buffet was spread. Remarks overheard were all complimentary. 'Mark did well for himself this time,' she heard one man say lightly to his neighbour as he forked up a succulent slice of ham. 'I wish my wife could turn her hand to a spread like this. Save me a small fortune!'

Saving money had not been the point of the exercise, Tessa could have told him. Mark never complained about bills, no matter how large. He was fortunate, of course, that he didn't have to live within a budget.

Dean cornered her in the utility room where she'd gone to take a few scraps to Corey who was billeted there for the evening.

'Seems I owe you rather more than just gratitude,' he proffered gruffly, bending down to pat the little animal. 'Mark denies any knowledge of the money deposited to my account. That leaves you as the only possible source.' For the first time since she had known him, there was a genuine ruefulness in the grey-blue eyes as he looked up at her. 'I never meant for you to fork out, Tessa. It never even occurred to me that you might have any money of your own.'

'Because you still believed I might have married Mark for his?' she queried lightly.

'If I did, that's past and gone.' He straightened up again, his expression devoid of all jauntiness. 'He's the luckiest man alive to have you—especially in comparison to Diane. I'm going to pay you back, of course. Every last penny!'

She said with purpose, 'Would you have felt as obligated if it had been Mark's money?'

A ghost of the old self-confident smile touched his lips. 'Maybe not. Family and all that.'

'I'm family too now,' she pointed out. 'Regard it as a sisterly gesture to get you started again.'

'Even after what I did?'

'You already apologised for that.' She donned a smile of her own. 'Anyway, perhaps I was a little too holier than thou.'

'Never!' He shook his head. 'I'll work something out. This job doesn't carry the world's highest salary, but it's a foothold to better things.'

'I'm sure it is.' Tessa hesitated before putting the question. 'Do you have any idea what happened to Fiona?'

'Was she invited?' He sounded surprised. 'I was under the impression there'd been a definite severance of association with the Leyland clan.'

Tessa looked at him sharply. 'She told you that?'

'More or less.' He laughed. 'Good thing I'd been planning on clearing out of her place, anyway, because I was given my marching orders.'

'When?' she asked.

He shrugged. 'A couple of days after we saw you at the restaurant. No explanation. Just get out and stay out!'

The same day she had visited Mark at the house, Tessa calculated. She felt confused. If Fiona had been angry enough to take it out on Dean that way, it could only have been because Mark hadn't come up to expectations in some way. Yet how did that tie in with his attitude since? Why would he have sent the woman an invitation at all if he had already severed their relationship?

Except that she didn't know he had, did she? He'd never even answered the question at the time.

'I think we'd better get back to the party,' she said, trying to stem the hope in her heart. Even if it were true that Fiona no longer figured in his life, he still didn't love her, Tessa. Not the way she wanted so desperately to be loved.

Mark was talking with a group of people in the hall when they came out from the kitchen. Meeting the level gaze, Tessa could sense the anger in him, although he appeared calm and easy enough on the surface. Obviously he hadn't liked learning that she had given his brother money, yet it had been her own to do as she liked with. One more matter that needed clearing up.

It was with mingled relief and trepidation that she said goodbye to the last of the guests around one-thirty. After helping clear away the worst of the debris, Laura and her mother followed their menfolk upstairs. Mark had turned down the opportunity for an earlier retirement and was ostensibly checking ashtrays. Waiting for the opportunity to say his piece, Tessa assumed.

He was standing with his back to the dying fire when she went through to the sitting-room, hands thrust deep into trouser pockets, jaw rock hard.

'I'll make arrangements first thing on Monday to have the two thousand transferred into your account,' he said tautly. 'And it stays there!'

'I don't want it.' She was resolute on that score. 'Dean will pay me back, given time.'

'That isn't the point.'

'I'm sorry,' she said, 'but I think it is. It's between him and me, no one else.'

'I see.' The tone was suddenly rougher. 'And I suppose you're going to make out it was a purely philanthropic gesture?'

Brown eyes refused to veer. 'Are you suggesting it could have been anything else?'

'Why not? You're not exactly averse to his company.'

'If you're talking about what I think you're talking about, we were feeding Corey through in the utility room,' she returned with dignity.

'You weren't feeding Corey the night I caught the two of you in a clinch!'

'That was already explained.'

'No, it wasn't explained. Glossed over, maybe.' He paused, the anger in him frightening in its intensity. 'Why should I trust *you* to be telling *me* the truth? It cuts both ways!'

'I know.' Her voice was low, her chest aching. 'I'm only just beginning to realise how easy it is to misread a situation. I don't have any feelings for Dean, Mark. Not the way you mean. I suppose, if anything, I was sorry for him. He had to have some kind of backing.'

'And you were so sure I wouldn't provide it?'

'All right, so I should have asked you first,' she agreed thickly. 'It just seemed easier to do it myself, that's all.'

'If that brother of mine had anything about him, he'd have asked me himself, instead of coming to you with his problems,' came the clipped response. 'Anyway, what I said still stands. The transfer will go through on Monday.'

It was hopeless arguing with him, she knew. The money wasn't the important issue, anyway. She said slowly, 'Mark, why wasn't Fiona here tonight?'

There was no visible change of expression. 'Probably because she wasn't invited.'

Tessa gazed at him, trying to read the mind behind the grey eyes. 'Why not?'

He smiled faintly. 'She wouldn't have appreciated the gesture.'

'I don't understand.'

'It's simple enough.' He was speaking quite calmly now, but the tension was still there in the set of his jaw. 'That day you saw her car at the door was the day I told her a few home truths. She didn't appreciate that, either.'

Something inside Tessa began to cautiously unfurl. 'You mean you finished with her as far back as that?'

He said something sharp under his breath, his whole stance hardening again. 'There was never anything to finish. Will you get that through your head? I saw her a couple of times during the fortnight before the wedding, yes. We were viewing properties—whittling down the possibles to the most likely for you to see after we got back. We had lunch together, even a drink or two. What I didn't do was sleep with her—either then or later.'

Tessa swallowed on the hard lump in her throat. 'Why didn't you tell me that when I asked?' she whispered.

'Because you didn't ask,' he said, 'you accused.' His shoulders lifted. 'All right, so maybe I over-reacted a little myself. Coming out of the blue at a time like that— well, enough to say I wanted to put you through it.'

'And since?' She could hardly get the words out.

'Same difference, I suppose. You had me down for the kind of louse who'd play that sort of game, so I played up to the image.'

'Oh.' She was so far down, she thought she would never come up again. 'Mark, what can I say?'

There was no relaxing of the lean features. 'You could start with something like "I believe you".'

'I do.' She tried to make it sound as sincere as she felt. 'I really do!'

'That's something, anyway.' He studied her for a moment, still not giving anything away. 'So, having finally got that cleared up, we'd better start giving some serious thought to where exactly we go from here.'

Her heart jerked painfully. 'Do you want me to go?'

'And leave Jason?' The smile had a wry quality. 'I never imagined the day might come when I'd be jealous of my own son!'

'Jealous?'

'That's what I said.' His own voice took on a sudden roughness. 'Have you any idea what it's like to know how much more you feel for him than you do for me?

I could share you with him, but I can't take being on the outside. Not any more. You're going to learn to love me too, Tessa, because I'm not willing to settle for anything less!'

She wanted to laugh and cry at the same time. This couldn't really be happening. Any moment she was going to waken up and find it had been another dream!

'It won't take a lifetime,' she said shakily. 'It won't even take a minute. I love you now, Mark. More than——'

She broke off there because he was coming across to her, pulling her to him with a look on his face that melted every last reservation she might have entertained. Lifting her face to him, she thrilled to the strength in him, to the overwhelming knowledge that everything was coming right with her world—with both their worlds. They were starting over again from this moment. No more misunderstandings. No more mistrust.

'Tell me again,' he said some time later when he had kissed her into a state when she hardly knew what time it was and didn't even care. His eyes were tender, his hands smoothing the tumbled hair from her face. 'Say it slowly so I can take it in.'

They had progressed to the nearest sofa. Held safe and secure in his arms, Tessa felt her cup was spilling over. 'I love you,' she told him, and saw the small twin flames kindle afresh.

'So what took you so long?' he demanded.

Her smile was tremulous. 'I was only scared to say it, not to feel it. I was in love with you when you asked me to marry you.'

'You didn't give me much sign of it. Physically attracted, yes. The same way I was.'

'Why?' she asked. 'I'm not beautiful like Fiona and Diane.'

'Eyes like brown velvet, skin like silk and a mouth I itched to kiss the very first time I laid eyes on you.' His voice was very soft. 'If that isn't beauty, I don't know what is! You have something the Fionas and Dianes of this world will never have, Tessa, and that's character. I discovered the real difference between wanting and loving the night you came to me, although it took me a little time to realise it. I've never missed anyone or anything as much as I missed you those two weeks we spent apart. I wanted to come and get you every single day!'

'Why didn't you tell me?'

'I planned to,' he said. 'On our wedding night. Then you flung that accusation in my face, and——' He paused, the lift of his shoulders an apt comment. 'No point in going over all that again.'

She said huskily, 'You don't really believe your financial status might have had any bearing on my agreeing to marry you, do you, Mark?'

'Is that what I said?' He sounded rueful. 'I certainly didn't pull any punches! No, of course I don't believe it. It was your integrity that first drew me to you—plus your spirit—your sense of humour.'

Her laugh was a little unsteady. 'You make me sound a real paragon!'

'Not altogether. You exacted a vicious revenge.'

'With the utmost difficulty.' The smile faltered as memory crowded in. 'Mark, I've been such a blind, jealous fool. I ruined our wedding night!'

'We both contributed to that débâcle,' he said. 'We'll go back next year and relive it—properly this time.'

'After we give Jason his first real taste of a holiday.' She met the grey eyes honestly. 'The way I feel about him and the way I feel about you are two very different things. He needs me.'

'You think I don't?' He drew her up to him again to press his lips to her temple, holding her there in the circle of his arms as if he never wanted to let her go. 'As I said before, I don't mind sharing you with him. I love him too.'

It was all working out, Tessa thought mistily, her dreams coming true at last. Only one question remained in mind. It wasn't important any more, but she put it anyway.

'Just as a matter of interest, what was Fiona really doing at the house that afternoon?'

'She was under the mistaken impression I might be open to a takeover bid. I disillusioned her.'

'How?'

'I told her I was in love with my wife and intending to stay that way. She left in high dudgeon, as the saying goes.' His grin was sudden and boyish. 'It's hard work being so darned irresistible!'

Tessa laughed with him, the happiness welling in her. 'You won't stay estranged from Dean, will you?' she begged. 'He's truly sorry for everything!'

'So he damned well needs to be.' He looked down at her with a smile in his eyes. 'You've a forgiving nature, Mrs Leyland.'

'Life's too short for bearing grudges,' she returned. 'I know that's a cliché, but it's worth bearing in mind. Who knows, he may even settle down and become a family man himself one of these fine days.'

'Stranger things have happened.' Mark smoothed her lips with a fingertip, the touch so tender it almost brought tears to her eyes. 'Let's go to bed,' he said softly. 'I've a whole lot to make up for.'

And he would do it magnificently, she knew.

Harlequin Presents®

Coming Next Month

**In April, Harlequin brings you the
world's most popular romance author**

JANET DAILEY

No Quarter Asked

Out of print since 1974!

After the tragic death of her father, Stacy's world is shattered. She
needs to get away by herself to sort things out. She leaves behind
her boyfriend, Carter Price, who wants to marry her. However, as
soon as she arrives at her rented cabin in Texas, Cord Harris, owner
of a large ranch, seems determined to get her to leave. When Stacy
has a fall and is injured, Cord reluctantly takes her to his own ranch.
Unknown to Stacy, Carter's father has written to Cord and asked
him to keep an eye on Stacy and try to convince her to return home.
After a few weeks there, in spite of Cord's hateful treatment that
involves her working as a ranch hand and the return of Lydia, his ex-
fiancée, by the time Carter comes to escort her back, Stacy knows
that she is in love with Cord and doesn't want to go.

**Watch for *Fiesta San Antonio* in July and
For Bitter or Worse in September.**

JDA-1

Have You Ever Wondered If You Could Write A Harlequin Novel?

Here's great news—Harlequin is offering a series of cassette tapes to help you do just that. Written by Harlequin editors, these tapes give practical advice on how to make your characters—and your story—come alive. There's a tape for each contemporary romance series Harlequin publishes.

Mail order only

All sales final

- -

TO: *Harlequin Reader Service*
Audiocassette Tape Offer
P.O. Box 1396
Buffalo, NY 14269-1396

I enclose a check/money order payable to HARLEQUIN READER SERVICE® for $9.70 ($8.95 plus 75¢ postage and handling) for EACH tape ordered for the total sum of $_____*
Please send:

- ☐ Romance and Presents
- ☐ American Romance
- ☐ Superromance

- ☐ Intrigue
- ☐ Temptation
- ☐ All five tapes ($38.80 total)

Signature_____
                                                            (please print clearly)
Name:_____

Address:_____

State:_____ Zip:_____

*Iowa and New York residents add appropriate sales tax.   AUDIO-H

This April, don't miss Harlequin's new Award of
Excellence title from

CAROLE MORTIMER

Award of Excellence

elusive as the unicorn

*When Eve Eden discovered that Adam
Gardener, successful art entrepreneur, was
searching for the legendary English artist, The
Unicorn, she nervously shied away. The Unicorn's
true identity hit too close to home....*

*Besides, Eve was rattled by Adam's
mesmerizing presence, especially in the light
of the ridiculous coincidence of their names—
and his determination to take advantage of it!
But Eve was already engaged to marry her
longtime friend, Paul.*

*Yet Eve found herself troubled by the different
choices Adam and Paul presented. If only the
answer to her dilemma didn't keep eluding her....*

HP1258-1